watcher

watcher

valerie sherrard

John Hersey High School
Academic Resource Center

DUNDURN PRESS
TORONTO

Editor: Allison Hirst
Design: Jennifer Scott
Printer: Webcom

Library and Archives Canada Cataloguing in Publication

Sherrard, Valerie
    Watcher / Valerie Sherrard.

ISBN 978-1-55488-431-5

    I. Title.

PS8587.H3867W38 2009   jC813'.6   C2009-903263-5

1   2   3   4   5   13   12   11   10   09

  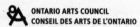

We acknowledge the support of the **Canada Council for the Arts** and the **Ontario Arts Council** for our publishing program. We also acknowledge the financial support of the **Government of Canada** through the **Book Publishing Industry Development Program** and **The Association for the Export of Canadian Books**, and the **Government of Ontario** through the **Ontario Book Publishers Tax Credit program**, and the **Ontario Media Development Corporation**.

Care has been taken to trace the ownership of copyright material used in this book. The author and the publisher welcome any information enabling them to rectify any references or credits in subsequent editions.

J. Kirk Howard, President

Printed and bound in Canada.
www.dundurn.com

Dundurn Press	Gazelle Book Services Limited	Dundurn Press
3 Church Street, Suite 500	White Cross Mills	2250 Military Road
Toronto, Ontario, Canada	High Town, Lancaster, England	Tonawanda, NY
M5E 1M2	LA1 4XS	U.S.A. 14150

Parental Alienation is a form of abuse
involving the destruction of a child's relationship
with one parent by the other.
It is, for the most part, an unpunished crime.
Those who pay the highest price are its victims:
the children,
who often become innocent participants.
Our courts have failed them.

This book is dedicated to those children.

Justice is truth in action.
— Benjamin Disraeli

prologue

I called him The Watcher.

He appeared to be in his early forties, casually dressed and basically nondescript-looking. I might never have noticed him except there were too many times that he was just *standing* around. I think that's what grabbed my eye. In the city, everyone seems to be in motion most of the time. Still, I think there was something else.

It could have been that kind of crawly feeling you get when you sense someone watching you. I caught him at it a couple of times, but usually when I swung my head around he'd be checking his watch or looking somewhere else or walking away without so much as a glance in my direction. I decided that he was slick, but no pro.

There was something familiar about him. I could never say exactly *what*, but it bugged me enough that I eventually ran it by Tack.

Tack, besides being my best friend, is definitely my oldest one. He's been around since I learned how to tie my own shoes. Back then we played together on the patch of ground that's supposed to pass for a lawn between our apartment buildings.

The yard might have had grass at some point in time, but not in my recollection. A few tufts jut up here and there but the rest of the surface is dirt that clearly has no intention of growing anything. You can tell, the way it's hard and pale, not rich and dark like the soil in the flowerbeds of classy neighbourhoods. You can find them anywhere. They're just a short subway ride and about a universe away.

Tack isn't his real name, by the way. You probably already guessed that. His actual name is Jeremiah, but the only person I've ever heard call him that is his mom. To the rest of the world, he's been Tack for as long as I can remember. Don't know how it got started, but it would be weird to call him anything else.

I'm tougher than Tack, though you wouldn't believe it if you saw us together. He has a good forty pounds and five inches on me, with all kinds of muscle and tone, while I look more like a pencil-necked techie.

I suppose we look funny when we hang out — Tack, tall and buff with his black skin glowing; me, thin and so white in contrast that I probably look as if I'm about to pass out.

I'm tough, though. You can ask anyone, and they'll tell you the same thing. I never bail out for any reason. I'd pick fight over flight any day of the week and never think twice about it. Matter of pride or honour — call it what you want, but I'll throw down with anybody, anytime.

Guys can tell, too. They can smell fear, taste it even, and if they catch so much as a hint, they'll circle you like a pack of wolves and tear you to shreds. But when they see that you're ready to stand, unafraid, almost *eager* to dig in, that makes them think.

Usually.

There are exceptions, and that can cost you. I've been hurt a few times, but I took three guys once and two another, and they paid for the damage they did to me.

Our apartment was on a Toronto street I'd rather not name, in an Ontario Housing complex. There was a "government-funded" look and a perpetual foul smell in the hallways, like somewhere in the building some-one was cooking cabbage every minute of the day. The apartments themselves weren't really that bad, but the only people we ever invited over were each other, by which I mean other occupants of the same collection of concrete boxes.

In a neighbourhood where the faces were constantly changing, it was a bit surprising that Tack and I had both been there for as long as we had. That was because our mothers were both single parents who'd found themselves trapped in the low-income cycle. They were always claiming that they were going to get out of there. As if that could ever happen without an action plan that goes past words.

Our fathers were what you'd call absent, though Tack saw his a couple of times that I can remember. The first time didn't go so well and he never mentioned the last visit. Not a word and I never asked. It's his story to tell when he gets it settled in his head.

My memories of my old man were kind of murky since my folks split up when I was pretty young. The year before I started kindergarten. The few memories I had of him weren't what you'd call pleasant. Mom always said we were much better off without him. She would say, "Who needs someone who left his family to rot on welfare for the rest of their lives?"

I knew one thing — I wasn't going to be rotting in that place the rest of *my* life. I was getting out of there. That place turned people into the living dead. I saw them everywhere, the ones who'd given up, their eyes emptied of hope. I was getting away from them, away from the yelling and crying that came at me through the thin walls, away from the sounds of despair — sounds that echoed like lingering ghosts on summer nights when it was too hot to sleep.

In that neighbourhood, it was hard to hear *anything* that didn't carry the sound of defeat.

I had it all figured out — my escape. And I'd learned something that was going to make a difference for me. I'd learned that knowing what you needed to do and actually *doing* it were two entirely different things. Sounds like something any idiot could figure out, doesn't it? That's what I thought, too.

The truth is, I didn't exactly get off to the best start. I spent a few years goofing off from school quite a lot. Started out maybe a couple of times a month, but it soon got to be two or three times a week. Not for whole days (usually) but a period here, an afternoon there. You know how it is.

I had better things to do than listen to a bunch of teachers drone on about stuff that was never going to matter to me. So, Tack and I had gotten into a bit of a habit you might call it, ditching classes and getting high out behind the dumpsters in back of our apartment buildings. We'd wait for our mothers to leave so we could sneak inside, kick back, and crank up some tunes.

Didn't seem like any kind of a problem. We managed to keep our mothers off our cases by staying a step or two ahead of them. Having an answer ready was the most important thing. If you were prepared, you were spared. That's how it worked for us, anyhow.

The main thing that saved us was that we could squeak by without failing or anything, and things might have just kept on that way if it hadn't been for a bit of a situation we got ourselves into.

It was one of those things that you do because you're not exactly thinking clearly. Not that I'm making excuses, but if we'd been straight, it might not have happened. We weren't straight, it did happen, and we got caught.

It was stupid, start to finish. We stuffed some CDs under our shirts in a little music shop near where we lived, and walked out. The owner was working that day. He saw us, knew who we were, and reported it. The cops stopped us before we even made it home.

Court was next. Not so bad for Tack because he was a first offender (though he got more than his share of trouble at home). He got community service and had to write an apology to the storeowner.

I got it worse because it wasn't my first offence. Or second. I'd had a couple of minor problems before that and the judge told me I'd run out of chances to prove I could straighten up on my own.

For the record, I really *wasn't* a criminal. The "previous convictions" that the Crown Prosecutor kept referring to when he was trying to persuade the judge I was some kind of big menace to society, were just a couple of pranks that caused a bit of damage. A broken bedroom window, a dent on someone's car fender, totally minor stuff. But, all of a sudden (with this CD thing) I found myself a three-time offender.

My mother was in court with me. She moved like someone fragmented — from fury to tears and back, finally settling on a state that managed to include both. Any second I failed to look sufficiently miserable and sorry for my deeds brought a glare, a hiss, and a wordless message that I was bringing shame and hurt to her.

It was way worse than the sentence.

"One year of supervised probation." It was a relief to hear this at last, after more than three hours of my mother's performance, and a long, harsh lecture from the judge that came out like a recitation.

I half expected him to wrap up with, "And may God have mercy on your soul."

That wasn't the turning point, but it shoved me toward it.

Anyway, I seem to have gotten a bit off track. I started out telling you about the guy who was watching me.

chapter one

Spring had just swept in, pushing out the winter with steady winds and the swollen kind of rain you only get at that time of year. The snow sizzled and shrank into itself. Huge white hills turned into withered, dirty mounds that finally disappeared, melting and joining the streams of water that pulsed along the streets.

I've always liked the spring. It's like the whole city is in a better mood then. Winter layers get peeled back — it's a kind of freedom.

This particular day, and I think it was a Saturday late in May but I'm not a hundred percent on that, I'd gotten up late. When I saw that it was drizzling outside I put on one of my mom's CDs. Her taste in music doesn't exactly agree with mine, but some of the stuff she has is okay. At least it's not what Tack's mom likes, which is old tunes so mournful and drawn out they'd have to cheer themselves up before you could call them the blues.

I had The Hip on, playing "Blow at High Dough" loud enough to feel it. It's a song you can't sit down to and I was on my feet moving across the living room floor like it was a stage. The second it ended I hit the repeat button on the remote, waited impatiently for the opening riffs to finish, and felt the pulse of the song rise up through me again.

"Well, I ain't no movie star," I howled, joining Gordon Downie on the second spin, "but I can get behind anything. Yeah, I can get behind anything."

That song always made me feel like I could. Get behind anything.

I became aware of Tack standing in the doorway about halfway through the second verse, which cut off my performance before the fans could get a full taste of my talent. I hit stop on the remote (which I might as well tell you had been doubling as a "microphone") and faced him.

"*What?*" I demanded. His face was just barely keeping a smirk under control.

"You need a drive somewhere?" he asked. "Like a Canadian Idol audition, maybe?"

"Why, did you bring your Saab?"

He shook his head sadly. "Trunk's too small."

"For what?"

"Not for your *talent*, that's for sure. But you can't be sittin' next to me like some kind of babe repellent."

At least he didn't call me repugnant, I thought. The previous weekend he'd watched *Jackie Brown* for about the fifth time, and since then everything had been repugnant to him. (Tack's a big Tarantino fan. He's seen all of his movies so many times he knows half the lines.)

"The ladies get a look at a skinny white dude like yourself," Tack went on, "you just *know* they got to find it repugnant."

There it was.

We spent the next few minutes deciding what to do, or, more accurately, where to go. There was never actually anything much to *do* most of the places we hung out, unless we happened to have some cash, which wasn't often. Mainly, we just kicked around and talked about things we were *going* to do someday.

Sometimes, if we had a few bucks we'd take the subway — get off at some random station, walk around a bit, and then head home, or somewhere else. We'd seen some pretty weird things, and not all of them in bad neighbourhoods.

Once, a couple of blocks from the stop at Yonge and Rosedale, we saw an old woman standing in the middle of the street singing in a high, squeaky voice.

The weird and, well, sad part was that she was wearing a housecoat and nothing else. That wouldn't even have been so bad if she'd had it done up, but she didn't. With every wave of her arm it fluttered open a little, revealing a body so thin she looked like a skeleton with some loose skin flapping. I swear I didn't want to look but I couldn't help myself. It was horrifying and fascinating all at once.

What it *wasn't* was one bit funny, so it really got me going a minute later when some kids — I'd say they were between nine and twelve — came along and started laughing and shouting things that aren't worth repeating.

I was torn then, because I'd have liked to smash them all — just one good pop each — but they *were* just kids. And, anyway, before I could react, Tack stepped out. I was pretty surprised, and curious to see what he might do.

The kids saw him coming, saw the look on his face, and suddenly decided they had somewhere else to be. They took off whooping and shrieking but he wasn't heading for them.

He reached the old gal just a minute or two before a tired-looking woman hurried out of a nearby house and headed toward her. Tack got there first and said something real quiet to the old woman. Then he tugged the housecoat together and did up a couple of buttons so fast I don't think she even knew it had happened.

She started to yell — a hollow, haunting sound that went on and on. By then the woman, probably either her daughter or daughter-in-law, had reached her. She said something to Tack, then took hold of the old gal's arm and talked gently to her as she led her away.

Tack shrugged but he looked sort of wounded. When he'd rejoined me on the sidewalk, I asked him what she'd said.

"She said I should be ashamed of myself."

"For *what*?" I was instantly enraged.

"Who knows, man? She don't know what went down. She just sees the old woman howlin' like a banshee, and I'm right there so she figures I done something wrong."

It seemed as if he'd brushed it off — like a bug of some sort — but you can't always tell with Tack. Lots of things have to set with him for a bit. I knew that had happened when we'd walked in silence for a while and all of a sudden he asked, "Think she woulda said the same thing to *you*?"

I knew what he was really asking, but I just said, "Yeah, probably."

A few more silent moments and then Tack asked, "Whaddya think was wrong with her? The old one?"

"Alzheimer's, I guess."

"Think she knows what just went down?" Tack looked worried.

"Nah, they don't remember stuff like that. I don't think they remember much of *anything* by the time they get to that point."

"So, her whole life is gone? Everything she ever done, erased outta her brain?"

I didn't answer. I didn't know the answer. And I could see by the look on his face that he wasn't really asking me. His eyes had drifted somewhere else.

I turned back toward the subway. Sometimes your own street is the best place to be.

We never got off the subway at Rosedale again. Didn't have to talk about it — we just didn't go back.

I'm not sure how I got into that whole story. I started telling you about the first time I saw The Watcher.

It was on the Saturday in May that I mentioned earlier and we'd ended up walking the paths in High Park once the rain had stopped. The park was one of Tack's favourite places. He liked to lie back on the grass on the side of a low hill and just stare at the sky. We'd talk about a lot of things — the Big Questions — there, with all that space around us. Tack used to say that the open fields and sky gave his thoughts room to float free.

On this day, we'd been out for the afternoon and we were both getting pretty hungry. We were heading for my place because my mom had made a macaroni casserole the day before. My sister and her boyfriend were supposed to come over but they hadn't shown up, so there was a lot left.

We'd reached the corner of our street and had walked right by an old guy — a street person — without even seeing him. But we stopped and turned toward him when he yelled out what sounded like, "Tack!"

It was an odd thing, to hear a heap of rags with legs splayed out at the bottom saying Tack's name.

"You talkin' to me?" Tack asked after a few seconds.

"Ah, Tack!" shouted the derelict.

"Yeah?" Tack said. He looked puzzled but he took a step toward the bum.

"Curse this mud!" cried the old fellow. "Can't walk, can't dig. We'll all die out here."

"I don't think he's talking to you," I observed.

"Ah! Tack!" The feeble yell came again.

"So, why's he sayin' my name?" Tack asked.

"I think he's saying *attack*, having some kind of flashback to the war," I told him. "I remember an old guy in my building talking about the mud the same way."

Tack looked a bit relieved. He also leaned down and told the poor man it was okay, that the mud was gone and the war was over.

It was impossible to tell if the old fellow even heard him. If he did, it made no difference. He kept on thrashing about and yelling.

But it was because of this encounter that I first noticed The Watcher. I think I'd seen him before that, without registering anything in particular about him. But stopping to talk to the old guy, I became aware of this man. He'd been coming along behind us but he'd faded into a store doorway when we stopped.

I still wouldn't have thought anything of it, but when we started walking again, he reappeared, back a ways but hanging steady behind us.

"Wonder where *he* come from," Tack said when we'd gone a short ways down the street.

"You see him too?" I asked, surprised.

"*See* him? Man, what's with you? Weren't we just *talkin'* to the man?"

"Oh, him. Yeah." I was about to explain about the guy who was following us, but just then he turned off the sidewalk toward an apartment building.

So, I figured it was a coincidence and put him out of my head.

Until the next time, that is.

chapter two

I didn't see The Watcher again for nearly a week. The derelict, on the other hand, was in the same place on the corner most of the time. The homeless tend to do that — claim certain spots.

The second time I saw the bum he wasn't raving about wars and fighting. He just sat there, staring ahead in an alcoholic stupor.

I stood for a minute or so, watching him. Watching to see if he was breathing, actually. That kind of state can be scary and if you've ever seen it you know what I mean. You'd almost swear they were dead, the way they sit with their eyes open but unfocused.

He was almost entirely still and his breathing was so shallow there was no chest movement that I could see, but I noticed that the small finger on his left hand was twitching slightly, as if it was conducting a musical no one else could hear. Like most street people, he was wearing layers of clothing in various stages of filth and decay, which was what made it seem as though he was dressed in rags. The soles of his shoes were worn right through in a few places and grey work socks that were in equally bad condition peeked out.

I shrugged and moved along. He wasn't my problem.

I really couldn't have cared less about the old guy. Even so, part of me got thinking about a pair of shoes Mom had picked up for a couple of bucks at one of those used clothing places. They were black with a thick rubber sole, and she'd tried to make me wear them to her friend Nabida's funeral. Said it was a sign of respect. Said I'd wear them or I wouldn't be going.

I didn't wear them. And I didn't go. I'd liked Nabida, too. She always talked to me normal, asked me what I thought about different things, and listened when I answered.

Nabida was one of the good ones. And I *would* have gone to her funeral — not that it mattered to her — but it turned out I didn't, because of those stupid shoes. They'd been sitting in the back of my closet ever since.

I found myself wondering if they'd fit the old guy. Then, thinking about giving him shoes started to embarrass me. After all, he was nobody and nothing to me. Just a bum who'd ruined whatever he used to have for a life. Why should I care if he had holes in his shoes? His misery wasn't my concern.

And anyway, I had homework — three pages of math — to do and I figured I'd better take a look at my biology book, too. There was a test coming up in a couple of days and I hadn't exactly aced the last one.

Thinking about the test and the mark I was getting in biology put me in a pretty bad mood. Even though it had no relation to the old guy whatsoever, I made my mind up that I was going to throw those stupid shoes out.

I yanked my closet door open, leaned down, and started looking for them. Things kind of got shoved around in there and sure enough the bottom was stuffed full. I pulled out objects one at a time — a broken Playstation, old school binders, a stuffed giraffe I used to sleep with when I was a kid (I've been meaning to throw that out), some old gym shoes, a skateboard with one wheel loose, a baseball and bat (my glove got lifted last year), and something wrapped in an old towel.

I pulled that out and it wasn't until I had the towel almost off that I remembered what was in it — a bong, shaped like a skull. It gave me a kind of weird feeling, holding it again. It had been a couple of years, and I wasn't even sure why I'd kept it. Maybe because of what it cost me.

It had been getting close to Christmas, back in grade eight, and Mom had given me some money to do a bit of shopping. She used to do that every year, so I could get something for her and my sister, Lynn, who was still living at home then.

I thought I might as well get it over with, and the sooner the better. It really didn't matter what I bought, the reactions were the same year after year.

Mom would go on way too much about how she *loved* whatever I'd given her. Lynn, on the other hand, would look like she couldn't quite *believe* anyone could possibly be a big enough moron to have picked out the present I'd gotten for her. Until Mom gave her the old prompt, that is.

"What do you say to your brother, Lynn?"

This would get me a phoney smile followed by a sing-song, "Thank you, Porter."

The pathetic thing was that every year I honestly tried to pick out something she'd like. She always got me something cool, something just right. It'd be expensive too and Mom would go on about how it must have taken months of babysitting money. (I never knew — or wanted to — exactly *how* Lynn got my gifts, but I was dead sure she wasn't buying them retail.)

By grade eight, I'd accepted the fact that no matter what I got for her, it wasn't going to be good enough.

I figured I'd take a quick look, grab the first thing that seemed halfway suitable, and be finished with the whole racket for another year.

But then I passed the old dry cleaning shop. It had closed down a couple of months before and I saw that there was a new business inside. Some kind of store. There was no sign or anything, but there were already a few things displayed in the window. The bong was one of them, but it was a statue, carved and partly painted, that first caught my eye. I couldn't tell if the mouth was laughing or howling and I stood there for a moment trying to decide.

"Come on in, mon," a soft voice said from the doorway. "We got what you want."

How would he know what I wanted? I wondered. But there was something hypnotic about the way he'd spoken and I found myself going in. I was halfway through the doorway when I noticed the bong, perched on a small round platform that was covered with a dark purple scarf.

It was a work of art. Skulls generally look pretty much the same but this one was unusual. It took me a few minutes to figure out why, and when I did, I knew I had to have it. There was something about it that made it look wise, as though it had the answer to every question ever asked, if only a person could get it to speak.

It wasn't like I thought it ever *would* talk. But there are strange things that happen in the world, things you can't explain. For all I knew, a person might pick something up from it by osmosis.

Looking at it in my room a couple of years later, I had no idea *what* I could possibly have thought was so special and magical about this thing. But back then, it seized me so hard it seemed as if I had no choice.

I asked how much it was. The guy gave me a price that was about three times what I had on me. I must have looked pretty disappointed, because he asked what I could afford. I told him the amount, to the last dime, that I had in my pocket.

"Maybe," he said with a slow, lazy smile, "we can work something out for the rest, mon."

chapter three

I'm no idiot. I knew right away that whatever he had in mind, it wasn't going to be something I'd want to hurry home and brag about to my mother. I thought it might be smart to clear out of there, but the guy was talking.

"Easy, mon," he was saying. "You don't hafta kill nobody — this time."

A big laugh followed that, and it pretty much went with the dreads and the way he was dressed, a deep laugh rising up from inside, an almost Santa style, "Oh, ho, ho, ho."

Only it was just a shade off.

I looked at him closer, really seeing him for the first time.

"Rodney?" I asked. He looked alarmed for a few seconds, and I think he was going to deny it, but then he changed his mind.

"Hey, Porter. I didn't recognize you." His shoulders rose and fell in a "what can you do?" shrug.

"What is *wrong* with you," I asked. "Did you forget where you were from or what?"

"It's just part of the, you know, *ambiance*, man," he said, waving his arm around the room. He looked embarrassed. "You got to look and sound the part."

I nodded toward the skull. "And what were you going to ask me to do for this?"

"Just help clean out the back room." He laughed, normally this time. "It's taking forever to get this place organized. You shoulda seen your face, though."

I hadn't seen Rodney for a couple of years, since before he finished school. He used to rule the skate park a couple of blocks away. He could make that board do anything. Showed me a few tricks, too, though not if anyone else was around.

"Clean out the room? That's it?"

"What did you think I wanted you to do? Sell crack to kindergarteners?"

"Something like that."

"Just so you know, this business is one hundred percent legit," he said. He looked offended.

"Yeah, well, I didn't know it was *you*," I said. "I thought I was talking to Bob Marley's second cousin."

He laughed good-naturedly, then asked, "So, do we

have a deal, or what?"

I said yeah, and he led me to the back room. It needed cleaning all right, but mostly it needed to be organized. There were stacks of papers and boxes — some opened and some still taped up — in haphazard piles everywhere. One look around told me I'd earn the rest of the price of the bong all right.

I spent a couple of hours that day, and went back a few more times before the room was done. I worked *hard*. Not only that, but I still had to find a way get those stupid Christmas gifts.

Like I said before, I'm no criminal. This was just one of those situations where I really didn't seem to have a choice. You know how it is.

So I stole them.

It was the first time I ever jacked something and I might as well admit I was pretty scared going in. I'd thought about asking Tack to come with me, but in the end it seemed like something I might want to keep to myself. I went alone to the nearest department store — the kind that they have big chains of — so it wasn't like I was putting some little old lady out of business.

The big problem, I realized right away, was that I felt out of place in the aisles with ladies' clothing, jewellery, candles, and things like that. Those sections aren't exactly overrun with teenage boys and I felt like I stuck out. My uneasiness made the chance of someone noticing me (okay, catching me) far more likely.

Two different salesladies asked if they could help me. I had a mental picture of them later on, discovering that something had been taken and calling the police, with a full description of this suspicious-looking kid they'd seen earlier.

If I'd been able to come up with some kind of story to cover for the missing money, I'd have turned around and walked right back out of the store then and there. But I couldn't. So, I fought back my fear and wandered around the place trying to look normal.

I've seen people shoplifting since then and I can tell you that the biggest giveaway is the way they're working at looking casual, just as I was doing that day. It's a hard act to pull off.

Luckily for me, no one seemed to be paying much attention to the skinny kid with the sweaty palms and the *too*-innocent face. I ended up with a sports watch for Lynn and a package of fancy stick-on fingernails for Mom. She was always saying how she'd love to have long nails.

Once I'd stuffed these two things inside my jacket, I had to fight to keep from bolting out the entrance and running. Walking toward the door was unbelievably hard, and when the alarm sounded I nearly passed out.

It was pure luck that a woman carrying a couple of shopping bags was going through the security machine at the same time. She stopped and looked expectantly at the cashier, who said, "The machine must not have scanned something right."

Amazingly, no one seemed to have even noticed me, although my legs had gone liquid and barely held me up as I shoved open the door and hit the pavement. I realized I was holding my breath.

I pushed my shaking hands into my jeans' pockets and swallowed a lungful of air. I moved along the sidewalk, unable to resist quickening my pace. Halfway along the length of what seemed the longest building in the world, I broke into a trot and then sped up, feeling the air rush cold against the sweat on my face.

I nearly puked when I got home. Even there, I didn't feel safe. It was hours before I stopped waiting for a knock on the door. I was dead sure I'd never steal anything again.

Through it all, the single thing that really seemed to matter was that I got that bong.

I stared at it, remembering how important it had seemed at that time, and now there it was, wrapped in a towel and tucked out of sight, totally useless to me.

Sure, I'd made lots of use of it back when I got it, and probably wouldn't have retired it at all if it wasn't for the scrape Tack and I had gotten into, and what had happened afterward.

I remembered how I'd used the bong a few times the weekend before court. It got rid of the worry and uneasiness — mellowed me out and turned my anxiety into a mix of indifference and amusement. I saw it as a problem solver, and I managed to believe it was nothing to worry about. It wasn't like I was cranking or anything.

Funny, looking at the bong that day, I could almost bring back that feeling of floating calm. The uneasy thought popped into my head that maybe I'd kept it "just in case."

I decided I'd spent enough time thinking about that, rewrapped it in the towel and shoved it into the back corner of the closet. I actually had to stop and think for a few seconds before I remembered what I was doing in there.

The shoes. Where were they anyway? I didn't remember throwing them out but then it had been a while. Maybe Mom had given them to someone — but she wouldn't have gone into my closet and I couldn't remember her asking for them.

I looked again and discovered that I'd missed an old gym bag, tucked off to the side and blending into the dark of the corner. When I pulled it out and managed to force the zipper open, I found the shoes in there, along with a few other things — none of which looked too attractive. The shoes had been keeping company with some crumpled old socks (apparently, they were ready for the washer when they were abandoned), a dried out stick of deodorant, a couple of empty Pepsi cans and a fuzzy green lump that disintegrated into a scary-looking cloud when I prodded it with the heel of one shoe.

I took the shoes to the bathroom and wiped them off with one of the rags Mom kept under the sink there. They seemed to have survived their time in exile without suffering any permanent damage. If they fit him, they'd sure be a help to the old guy.

That was when it hit me that my original intention when I'd started hunting for them was to throw them out. Only, I couldn't remember why.

chapter four

The second time I saw The Watcher was the day I took the shoes to the bum. He was sitting there in "his" spot like an unsightly fixture, mumbling and fluttering his hands. It looked like he was trying to wave his arms around, but just didn't have the energy for it.

I don't know if there was any sense to what he was saying, but it's not likely. If you've been around many street people you know what I mean. They tend to talk continuously and it doesn't take long until you get to the point that you don't bother trying to follow what they're saying. Or trying to say.

Fact is, a lot of their talk is angry — kind of outraged and protesting. Most of them seem to be complaining about something. Only, no one is listening.

They don't bother me, except for the arm grabbers. That's one thing I just won't put up with, someone grappling on to me. Last time a bag lady came up to me and took hold of my arm with her gnarled and dirty hand, I almost shoved her. It would have taken her off her feet and I wouldn't have wanted that, but sometimes you react to things automatically.

As it was, I just stopped myself in time. I yanked away from her and walked off while she screeched that her niece had taken everything.

Maybe her niece *had* taken everything. Maybe she'd robbed her blind and turned her out into the street. Or, maybe she borrowed a punch bowl once and never brought it back. Or, maybe the old woman didn't even *have* a niece. That's the problem with stories from people on the street. You don't know if they're based on reality or if they're tortured inventions creeping out of minds that have been twisted by some mental condition or too many binges.

The guy I took the shoes to that day was mumbling again, but this time it wasn't about the war. I didn't wait long to see whether or not he was connected to the real world at the moment. I just leaned down and told him I'd brought him shoes.

He kind of focused for a minute, looking at me like he was trying to puzzle out who I was and why I was talking to him. I held the shoes up where he could see them, said, "These are for you," and put them in his lap.

He stared down at them uncomprehendingly at first and then, slowly, his face took on a look of understanding. His feeble hands trembled as they slid off his old shoes and pulled the new ones on. Suddenly, he began to smile and for a second he didn't look quite so pathetic.

I found myself smiling, too, which made me feel foolish, so I walked away, down to the corner store for a bottle of Pepsi. Then I headed back home. That was when I saw The Watcher for the second time.

He was looking out the window of Suleiman's, a restaurant on the corner where I turn onto my street. I thought at first that he was at a table, having a bite to eat or a cup of coffee or whatever. Only he wasn't. He was just leaning down, peering out between the images of falafel and stuffed vine leaves that are painted on the window. He looked away quickly when he realized I'd spotted him.

I still might have dismissed it if nothing else had happened that day. I could have convinced myself that he'd been in there to order take-out or maybe to meet someone who hadn't shown up yet. Any number of things could have made him look out the window. And if he just happened to look in my direction, well, so what?

Except that wasn't the end of it. Later on, I was heading over to Tack's place and there he was again! This time he was up ahead, pretending to be waiting for the streetcar. I saw him look at me and then act as if he was trying to see something behind me.

I picked up the pace a bit so I could get by and out of his sight, not because I was scared but because I didn't like the idea of this guy up in my business. I shot him a penetrating look as I came up on him. That startled him and I almost stopped and said a few things to set him straight, but the streetcar was pulling up. He hesitated, but then he had no choice but to go ahead and get on it.

I saw him, plain as day, leaning over and looking straight at me as the streetcar pulled away. I stared right back at him, careful to keep my face blank. There was no way I wanted him to think he was getting to me.

Anyway, there'd be other opportunities to deal with him face-to-face. Whatever this guy's game was, he wasn't exactly the slickest player in town. It was possible that he'd been following me — watching me for longer than I knew. But since I'd caught him at it a couple of times in the past week alone, and now that I knew I was being watched, it would be almost impossible for him to do it without me seeing him.

I was thinking about this as I got close to Tack's building. Then I heard someone behind me say my name.

"Yo! Porter!"

I spun around, startled. "Tack. I didn't see you, man."

"Maybe 'cause you look like you're in a trance, dude. Like the hypnotist got you."

I said nothing about The Watcher. *I* knew it was true, but I wasn't sure I could convince Tack without more proof.

"I was just thinking about something," I said vaguely. Then, to change subjects, I suggested we go to his place.

That brought a reaction I wasn't quite expecting. He threw both hands up like he was surrendering and told me *no way* were we going there. Apparently, his mother was going to kill someone this time *for sure*, and he'd just ducked out before she could decide it should be him.

"Why?" I laughed, picturing his mother on one of her rampages. "What happened?"

"Oh, man ... who knows?" he said. He looked away.

"Yeah, right." I laughed. There was guilt written all over his face. "I'm betting *you* know. And I think whatever it is, *you did it*."

Tack glanced behind him nervously, like someone might be listening.

"I don't remember her sayin' nothin' about that last chunk of mudslide bein' hers," he muttered.

"You ate *your mother's* piece of cake?" I took a step to the side. "Get away from me, man. I don't want to get hit by the fallout."

This wasn't Tack's first transgression in the food department. Not long ago he'd gotten into a pie his mother had made for some ladies' meeting at her church. She'd hidden it, or so she thought, in a plastic container up in the back of the cupboard over the fridge. It was no match for Tack, who'd sniffed it out and helped himself to a generous slice. I'd had the misfortune of being there when she came home and discovered it had been plundered.

All things considered, I didn't blame Tack for looking nervous now. His mother is a big woman (substantial, she says) and when she's wound up — man, watch out! Seeing her stomp and wave her arms and listening to her rant is something I can't quite describe. It's comical and scary all at once, but I'll tell you this much: you wouldn't open your mouth to talk back when she's in that kind of frenzy.

Tack told me once that when his mother gets going she puts him in mind of a southern preacher frothing and pacing onstage, shouting about vexation and damnation, except her messages are more for the here and now. According to Tack, the only reason she hasn't yet threatened him with hellfire is because she doesn't know where to get it.

I took pity on him and changed the subject.

By then we'd reached my place and were in the kitchen. Seemed that having his life endangered for eating forbidden food had given Tack an appetite. He asked right away if there was anything to snack on. I got some bread and peanut butter out, along with a couple of knives. We don't bother with plates unless my mom is around to insist.

"Want jam?" I asked.

"Got any grape jelly?"

I looked. There was none. He settled for strawberry jam, and we put together a couple of sandwiches and flopped on the couch to eat them.

That was when my sister Lynn came storming through the door, bawling her eyes out.

chapter five

The sight of my sister sobbing alarmed me, but not because of any worry over what might be wrong with her. I'd seen her bawling enough times through the years that I'd become immune to it by then. My main concern was that she might waste a bunch of my time with some stupid story about the latest fight between her and her boyfriend, Conor Sweeney.

The main thing to remember in that kind of situation is that you should act like you care without encouraging too much talk.

"It'll be okay," I said. You have to say *something*.

"N...n...no, it wo...wo...won't," she blubbered.

It takes experience to learn how to shut this kind of drama down as fast as possible. I had plenty of practice. The problem: Tack had none.

I saw him shift in his chair and turn to face her. I saw his mouth start to open — saw it like it was happening in slow motion. I knew he was going to say something and that whatever it was, it would be the wrong thing.

Sadly, I was powerless to stop him.

"What's wrong, Lynn?"

A long, tortured *NOOOOOOOOOO* echoed in my head. Too late.

"I...I b...b...broke up with C...Con...or." This brought on renewed hysterics.

(Every time they break up she claims *she* did the dumping, which is not even close to the truth.)

Tack blundered on.

"Aw, that's too bad," he told her. I silently willed him *not* to ask what happened, so of course the next words out of his mouth were "What went down?"

You'd almost wonder how a person could get to be Tack's age without knowing better than that. Sure, he's only got brothers, but he should have learned *something* from the girls he's gone out with. From what I've seen, they all operate pretty much the same.

It took all of my willpower to keep from snorting or rolling my eyes or doing anything else to make what was coming worse.

"Conor," Lynn said through her sobs and tears, "forgot the anniversary of our first kiss."

Tack looked confused. Why wouldn't he? He was probably thinking, *That's it? All this wailing and wet-eye is because the poor sap forgot a stupid date?* Thankfully, he didn't say anything like that out loud.

Lynn reached into her purse, brought out a package of Kleenex, tugged one out and blew her nose. Then she was ready to go on.

"I'm sure you can imagine how *awful* that made me feel, Tack. I was just devastated."

Tack looked like a cornered animal. His eyes darted to the left and right, but there was no way out. He mumbled something that sounded like, "Rats tube hat." I wasn't sure if I'd misheard, or if he was too panicked to form a sentence.

"I knew that if Conor could forget something that important, our relationship was in serious trouble." Lynn dabbed at her eyes with a fresh Kleenex. "To be honest, I should have seen this coming. I've felt us growing apart — women can sense these things. And we really hadn't been working on our relationship the way we should have been.

"But the worst part is, it tells me Conor doesn't really care. Not the way I do."

"Aw, now, sure he does," Tack said, because he didn't know any better.

"He *doesn't*" Lynn blubbered. "Don't you *see*! If he cared, our anniversary would be just as important to

valerie sherrard

him as it is to *me*. But it's not, and he doesn't and now I have to somehow find the strength to pick up the pieces and go on ... alone."

Tack shot a pleading look my way. It was so forlorn that I nearly stepped in to help him, but then I realized I was kind of enjoying watching him squirm, so I let it go.

"You know what the worst part is?" Lynn asked. Apparently, she'd forgotten that she'd just covered that.

"Uh, what?" Tack said in a doomed voice.

Lynn turned her red, swollen eyes toward Tack like he was her only hope. "The worst part was that Conor didn't even *know* what I was feeling!"

More sobs. More nose-honking into Kleenex. More wild-eyed looks from Tack.

"Didn't you *tell* him?" Tack asked. Another rookie mistake.

Lynn looked incredulous. "Oh, that is *so* typical," she said bitterly. "I shouldn't have to tell my own boyfriend these things. I shouldn't have to explain the difference between when I'm mad and when I'm sad. If our relationship was solid, he would know without being told."

"Oh," Tack said. I think he was catching on that the less he said, the better.

"I don't know why I get so upset over these things,"

45

she said, her shoulders convulsing. "I think it's because I'm just too sensitive sometimes."

"Nuthin' wrong with that," Tack assured her.

"Am I so terrible to want to have the kind of relationship where two people are so in sync with each other that they know each other's thoughts and feelings without being told? Is that so *wrong* of me?"

"Course not," Tack told her. His face told me he meant it. He didn't think she was wrong — he thought she was nuts.

"But I'm to blame too," Lynn said sorrowfully. "Maybe not as much as Conor — but in a way, what happened is my fault too."

Tack stayed silent. I mentally gave him a gold star.

"Because I," — sniff, sniff — "Well, I shouldn't say the things I say. I say *terrible* things to Conor when I'm hurting, and I know that, even though *he* hurt *me* first, he didn't *mean* to. I have to learn to let it go."

"Well, you know, nobody can do right every minute," Tack consoled. The error alarm in my head went off like mad. I mentally snatched the gold star back.

"So, you think I *was* wrong —" Lynn lifted her chin and looked right at Tack, looked at him like she was taking his measure, the way guys do to each other when they're about to mess it up.

"No, no. Not like that, you know."

"Come on, be honest. You think *I* messed up! You think it was wrong of *me* to get upset at *Conor* after he was just, like, *totally insensitive* to my feelings."

Tack did what he should have done right from the beginning. He threw up his hands, shut his mouth, and backed off.

It didn't take Lynn thirty seconds to see that she'd lost her opponent. As I knew she would, she whirled on me.

"What am I going to do?" she moaned, deflating from the bitter disappointment that the argument, that had seemed so promising, hadn't materialized after all.

"It'll be okay," I said in a monotone. I was determined to shut her down as fast as I could. Maybe Tack would pick up a couple of pointers.

But Lynn had already moved on. She looked at me with her eyes all sad and pleading and said, "Do you think that maybe you could, you know, talk to him?"

It almost always came to this moment, and when it did, I'd refuse in such a way that Lynn *knew* there was no negotiating. I'd make it totally clear that nothing she could say or do would change my answer — I simply could *not* be swayed, pressured, or pestered into it. Except, I always was. No matter how determined I'd start out, she'd wear me down.

So, this time I thought, why not take a shortcut and just do it?

"*No way*," I said. Because I still had to live with myself.

An hour or more later, after I'd given Conor a call and humiliated myself once again, after he'd sighed and told me to put her on the phone, after they'd talked and patched things up and she'd left, I turned to Tack.

"Man," I said, embarrassed that he'd seen my sister make me do something against my will, "Look what you got me into!"

"Don't be blamin' me!" he said indignantly. "It ain't *my* fault your sister's crazy."

And you know what — he was right. That wasn't his fault.

chapter six

A few weeks later we were adjusting to school being out for the summer, and talking, as usual, about finding jobs. When we passed by The Singing Cane (the store where I'd bought the bong a few years back), Tack suggested we go in and see if Rodney might happen to be looking for someone to work. We're always trying to make a few bucks, but in this case I think Tack really just wanted to check out what was new in there.

We went inside and looked around a bit while Rodney talked to a customer — a woman around my mother's age. I heard her saying she wanted to buy something unique for a friend's housewarming.

"Something a bit daring," she explained. Her voice dropped to a whisper. "I was thinking Rastafarian."

Rodney, complete with his "Jamaican" accent, humoured her as she giggled like she'd just said something naughty. He led her to some overpriced stuff that was no more Rastafarian than I am. The display was made up of items they probably sell to tourists in Jamaica, the kind of things that look — but aren't quite — representative of their actual culture.

The commercial stuff he stocks at The Singing Cane is cool but it's missing the peaceful focus of the whole Rastafarian philosophy. You'd have to look hard at Rodney's merchandise to find even so much as a hint of, you know, 'One Love.'

Anyway, the lady bought a wooden carving — ebony with bright slashes of colour on it — the kind that hangs on the wall. She seemed happy with it and I figured that, along with a unique present for her friend, she'd probably have a pretty good story worked up about the store and the Jamaican guy who'd waited on her. I guess that gave her her money's worth, one way or another.

"Hey, guys." Rodney turned to us once she'd hit the sidewalk. "What's goin' on?"

"Just hangin,' *mon*," Tack said, hiding a smirk. We tried not to ride Rodney too hard about the act but it was impossible to resist a small jab once in a while.

We yakked for a bit and then I brought up the subject of jobs.

"I'm not making enough money to hire regular help

yet," he said, shaking his head. "Sales are okay, but there's a lot going out, too. Operational costs, you know."

We said sure, like we knew all about operational costs. Then Rodney mentioned that there was a place nearby where he thought they might be looking for help, and suggested we check it out.

Turned out he was talking about a bakery that was just a few doors down. It didn't seem likely that they'd be all that interested in either of us, since we knew nothing about baking, but we went in anyway.

Behind the counter stood a girl who looked to be pretty close to our age, but I'd never noticed her around school. That was odd because she definitely wasn't someone you'd miss. She was gorgeous, with dark hair and eyes and glowing skin. In my side vision, I saw Tack straighten up a bit — kind of push his shoulders back and tighten up his gut.

"Yes?" she said shyly, after a quick glance at us.

"We're looking for the owner," I said. Tack confirmed this by smiling and nodding and smiling some more.

"Yes. My aunt. You will wait one moment please." She turned and went through a doorway into a back room. Tack let out a barely audible moan as she disappeared out of sight.

"I am Dunja Jankovich." The announcement came with the arrival of an older woman — the aunt, we presumed, although there was no resemblance that I could see. The young girl came back out behind her but didn't look in our direction again. Instead, she bent down and began arranging pastries in the glass display cases.

"We heard you might be looking for help," I said.

"You work in bakery before?" she demanded. Her eyes were narrowing, like she saw something sinister in us and thought maybe squinting would help her see it better.

"Not exactly," I said stupidly. I realized that sort of implied that we'd done something related to baking but there didn't seem to be any way to correct that without sounding like an idiot.

"You have résumé?" she asked next. Of course we didn't, since the whole job search had started on impulse.

"Uh, ma'am?" Tack said suddenly. "We thought maybe we could, uh, volunteer for a few weeks. If we learn good, you hire us."

"You work for nothing?" She grasped the idea pretty fast for someone whose English seemed a bit shaky.

"Yeah, for free. So you can see if you want to hire us." Tack offered a huge smile.

"H'okay. You start on Saturday morning. Come early. Five o'clock. I see how it goes."

He told her we'd be there like she'd just hired him for a twenty-dollar-an-hour job. I was too stunned to say a word.

We were out of earshot of the place before I found my voice.

"What, exactly, did you think you were doing back there?"

"What? With the volunteering?" Tack seemed genuinely puzzled.

"Of course *with the volunteering*."

"Be a good chance for, you know, on-the-job-training," he said without looking at me.

"Might be, but that's not why you decided to offer *our* services, is it, Tack?" I looked hard at him but he stayed focused on the sidewalk. "It's because of the girl, isn't it?"

"C'mon, man. It ain't that way," he protested.

"No? What way is it then? Tell me — exactly what was the force that drove you to tell Dunka that *we* — and by the way, *I'm* not doing it — would spend our Saturdays, starting *at five in the morning*, making cakes or whatever it is we'd be stuck doing?"

"Dunja," Tack said.

"Huh?"

"Dunja, not Dunka."

"Whatever." It didn't take much brainpower to see he was trying to avoid the real issue. Well, I wasn't letting him off that easy.

"Didn't seem like a big deal," Tack said at last. He looked embarrassed but his voice was defiant.

I shook my head but I didn't say anything else. I figured he'd got the message: he'd let his thinking get skewed by the girl and we both knew it. And, suddenly, I wasn't mad anymore. There was no point in pushing it any further.

We walked in silence for a ways, until I actually started feeling kind of sorry for coming down on Tack that way. I mean, it's not **like** we'd signed a contract or anything.

And I know what it's like when you meet someone who really hits you hard like that. It throws your brain totally out of whack.

I got thinking about that and had to admit there'd been a few occasions when I'd done really dumb things over girls myself. Not that we need to get into details.

"Okay, I'll go a couple of times, but that's it," I said after a while, like we were still right in the middle of talking about it. Pretty generous of me, I thought, letting Tack know that I understood and was, you know, there for him.

"Cool," he said, like he was granting me permission. No sign of appreciation.

I let that go, too.

There was a time when I let *nothing* go, but I've mellowed out a lot since I started looking at life differently. Basically, that goes back to the last time I went to court.

The sentence — a year of supervised probation — had sounded like a joke to me. I figured: big deal. I'll have to show up in some geek's office once in a while and say that I'm staying out of trouble. So what?

Of course, that was before I met Andrew Daniels.

chapter seven

He'd been in court the day I was sentenced, though I'd never have pegged him as a P.O. I'd noticed him earlier, sitting near the front, scribbling on a lined pad, and had figured him as a reporter having a slow day, or maybe a law student doing some kind of assignment.

After my sentence was passed, I was told to have a seat until the recess and to see my probation officer, Mr. Daniels, at that time so he could have me sign some papers before I left. That was when he turned and caught my eye and made a gesture that told me he was the guy the judge was talking about. I think my mouth fell open.

I'd had an idea in the back of my mind about what a P.O. would look like, and he definitely wasn't it. He hardly seemed old enough, for one thing. I mean, most of the people he'd be dealing with had to be a lot older — and tougher — than him. I could just picture him telling some scarred and muscle-bound thug what to do. Someone like that could crush him with one finger.

There was more than that, though. He looked so, I dunno, laid back and unconcerned. You'd think someone whose job was to try to get criminals to change their ways would be harsh and fierce — ready to come down hard and fast on anyone who messed up. Daniels had an air about him like he couldn't care less who broke the law or how often.

This impression wasn't altered by my first encounter, which lasted as long as it took for him to say, "Sign here," on my order, pass me an appointment card, and tell me he'd see me the next week.

"Oh, and let me know if you can't make it," he added in a tone that clearly said it didn't particularly matter to him one way or the other.

My appointment was scheduled for the next Tuesday, right after school. I got there a few minutes late and the secretary told me to go right in.

Daniels glanced up from his computer when I reached his office and stopped in the doorway. He nodded toward a pair of chairs facing the desk where he sat, and at the same time he swung the monitor up and out of the way. As I slid into the chair closest to the door, I saw that there was a file on his desk. My name was typed on an orange tag in one corner.

"Okay, Porter," he said, "this is our first meeting, so I'm basically going to tell you the way things work. You check in with me once a week — and we might get that down to a couple of times a month — for the next year, or until you get into more trouble. When that happens, you go back to court, and if there are changes to your sentence, we take it from there. Sometimes the next step is some kind of custody — open or even closed, sometimes you get another break and stay with the supervised probation program."

"You sound like it's a sure thing ... that I'm going to get into trouble again," I said.

"Yeah, so?"

"Well, I'm not."

"Sure, okay." He leaned back in his chair and looked at me, bending his arms and clasping his hands behind his head at the same time.

"I'm *not*," I repeated. His attitude really bugged me.

"Yeah? So, what's different then?" he asked.

"What do you mean?"

"You look like you're probably a stoner. You ditch a lot of school. I was just curious. What is it that's going to change the course you're on?"

"I'm not a stoner," I said. I was angry.

"Right. You just smoke dope on the weekends, and sometimes through the week. Maybe during school hours once in a while, but not enough for it to be a problem."

My mouth had gone dry listening to him. How did he *know* this stuff? It was so dead on that I was getting half spooked.

"Look, none of that makes any difference to me," he said. "Just keep your appointments. That's all I expect."

It sounded like he was telling me we were done, which was another shock. I'd gone there wondering if there was some excuse I could make to leave if it dragged on for more than half an hour. Instead, it looked like he was dismissing me after less than five minutes.

"Okay," he said, flipping open a book. "Let's see, next Wednesday. Four o'clock. Any reason that's not good for you?"

I told him there wasn't. He scribbled the time and date on a card and passed it over the desk. I wasn't even at the doorway before he'd gone back to whatever he'd been doing on the computer when I got there.

I was furious when I left. Who did this guy think he was, acting like he knew all about me? The bit about what would happen *when* (not *if*) I got into more trouble fed my anger.

But, then, I told myself there was no sense in getting all bent out of shape over it. If I had to put up with the jerk for the next year, it would be in my own best interest to stay cool. On the plus side, it looked like he wouldn't be wasting much of my time.

My next three meetings with Daniels went pretty smoothly. In and out, really. He'd ask how things were going and I'd say they were going okay. Then he'd add, like an afterthought, "No problems?" and I'd say "Nope," and that would pretty much be it.

But then there *was* a problem.

Word got out that one of the kids at school — Ghazi Havira, was going to have the house to himself for the weekend, while his parents were away. It meant a party — no way around it, though Ghazi himself didn't seem too enthusiastic about the idea. We might have made it hard for him to say no. I heard Johnny Dunlop make some crazy promise that everyone would help clean up, and that Ghazi's parents wouldn't even be able to tell anyone had been there. Like *that* had *ever* happened in the history of teenage parties.

The poor guy finally agreed to it when he was assured there would just be a *few* people coming over. You know the rest. By the time I got there things were just heating up and the place already looked like a war zone — assuming the other side was winning.

Ghazi had, as usually happens, reached a place well past caring somewhere along the line. He was drowning out what was going on around him with an interesting combination of rum and wine — a glass in each hand. When someone tripped and crashed through a glass end table, he looked over with barely focused eyes and shrugged.

I might have felt bad for him but I was pretty wasted myself and that would have bummed me out, so when the broken table turned from an accident into a free-for-all smash-fest, I just rode the wave. It kind of blurs at that point — I'd had a few drinks after smoking a thumbnail-sized piece of hash — but I vaguely remember stomping on a couple of statue-type ornaments that were on the floor. I can't swear to it, but I'm pretty sure they were already broken.

You have to realize that at this point *everyone* was laughing and smashing things. Well, almost everyone. I noticed that Ghazi had stopped looking dazed and started crying, huddled in a heap along one wall. Both of his drinks were long gone, the glasses part of the growing debris.

And then, as suddenly as it started, it was over. The last couple of morons to keep it up were quickly frozen out by the spreading shock and horror. For a minute or two no one looked at anyone. Then the exodus started.

I'd been travelling by myself that night and it didn't take me long to get out of there. I mean, I felt bad for Ghazi, sure, but there was nothing I could do about it.

He wasn't at school on Monday. Probably his parents weren't finished yelling yet. Tuesday he was back and I have to admit I felt a surge of relief when I saw him in the hallway. In a situation like that, you never know — a person could do something really stupid.

I tried to say hi to him in the hall but he turned his head and kept walking. I didn't blame him. Not then.

But Thursday that week, when I had my appointment with Andrew Daniels, that changed.

We went through the usual small talk, I answered his questions like I always did, and then he asked me, for the second time, "No problems? Nothing?"

A bad feeling started up in me, but I kept my chin level, looked him right in the eye and said, "Nope. Everything's cool."

Except, apparently, he'd heard otherwise.

chapter eight

"So, then, you didn't take part in trashing someone's house on the weekend?"

You'd think someone asking a question like that would have a bit of "pounce" in their voice, but not Daniels. His tone was as even and casual as always. If anything, he sounded a bit bored.

"Oh, well, if you mean what happened at Havira's place, I wasn't really involved in that."

"But you were there?"

"Uh, for a few minutes. I just stopped by ... looking for someone. Things had gotten pretty crazy, so I left."

"Uh-huh."

I couldn't tell if he believed me or not but I figured chances were good that he didn't. He just sat and looked at me, like he was waiting. I, on the other hand, tried to figure out how he knew about the party in the first place, and exactly what he might have heard about me.

"I suppose you're wondering," he said, like he was reading my mind, "how I heard about this party, or the fact that you were there."

"Not really," I lied.

"No? Well, then, I won't waste your time with the details," he said. He leaned forward and started to scribble something on a notepad in front of him. A desk calendar blocked my view but I was curious (okay, and nervous) to see what he was writing, so I shifted sideways like I was stretching, and strained to see it.

Daniels flipped the pad over just as I got the first words in sight. "So," he said, "that's it? You've got nothing else to say about this? Because, kid, other people are saying *plenty*."

"About *me*?" I could hardly believe it. I had no enemies; there was no reason anyone would want to pin this thing on me.

"Funny thing about that," he said. "It just happens that, of everyone at that party, *you're* the one who has a record. Is that pretty common knowledge among your friends?"

"I guess."

"So, Porter, you can see what happened. Kid's parents come home and find the place destroyed — and I guess it was bad all right. The only thing he can do is try to shift the blame off himself. Only, if I'm guessing right, he probably doesn't even *know* how it all happened. So he does the only thing he can do — he names anyone he can think of who already has a bad reputation."

"I don't have a bad reputation," I said, thinking of some of the kids I know who go around wrecking things for something to do. I was nothing like them.

"You have a *criminal record*, cat," he said. "Which is why I ended up getting a call from the homeowners on Monday. That was the day after they called the police, by the way. You can bet everything you own that your name was mentioned in that report, too."

For the first time since I'd been sentenced, I felt scared. Daniels had already told me I could be looking at custody time if I messed up again. Only, I knew I really didn't deserve the blame for the Havira's place. And I sure didn't want to end up in some detention centre with a bunch of older guys who thought they had something to prove.

Daniels was sitting there, quiet, watching me ... waiting.

"Look," I said, "I *swear*, what happened at that party wasn't my fault. I was just there, man. Someone fell on the end table and it broke and then the whole place just went crazy. I might have, you know, stepped on some broken glass or something, but I didn't start anything and I didn't bust anything up myself."

"What were you doing there in the first place?"

"Huh?"

"You were stoned, or drunk, or both. Either before you went or after you got there, right?"

I didn't answer.

"This is exactly why I give all you punks the same spiel when you come in. It's never a matter of *if* you're going to screw up. It's a matter of *when*. Because you keep getting high, you keep ditching school, you keep doing all the stupid, punk things that landed you in court in the first place."

I said nothing.

"If you weren't a doper, you wouldn't even have been at that party, would you?"

"No," I said. Oddly, a feeling of relief settled on me in admitting it.

"If I asked you what you were going to do with your life, you'd probably tell me finish school, get a decent job, buy a car and a house ... stuff like that, am I right?"

"I guess."

"Except, none of that is going to happen for you. You'll drop out, get into more serious crimes and end up in and out of prison for the next twenty or thirty years.

And none of that is what you *want*, but it'll happen sure as I'm sitting here."

"Well, isn't your job, I mean, aren't you supposed to *help* me?" I asked, angry.

"How? How am I supposed to help you?"

"You know, help me stay out of trouble."

"Why? Are you mentally deficient or something? Are you telling me that you don't know *exactly* what you need to do?"

I felt warmth crawling up my neck and onto my face, and I knew I was turning red.

"You don't already *know* that you need to quit using dope and stay in school?"

"I guess," I said.

"So, if you *know* it, and you're not *doing* it, I guess you want the life I just described. And, kid, you're well on your way. This new charge is going to get you off the streets, put you somewhere that you'll *really* get an education, and I don't mean academic."

"But I didn't do it," I said. My throat felt like it was trying to close up on me.

"Weird thing," he said, exhaling hard, "is I believe you. But I don't feel like sticking my neck out to help you, because there's no point to it."

"You mean you *could* do something?"

"Forget it. It's not worth the bother. Maybe you

didn't do this, but something else will come along. The end result will be the same. I'm not wasting my time for a punk like you."

"You wouldn't be," I said desperately. "I'll straighten up. I mean it."

He looked at me and for a second I thought he was going to laugh. Only he didn't. He sat quiet and I could almost see him weighing it all out. And I saw his eyes soften and drift while he was thinking, and then it was like he pulled back, and they started to get hard again.

"*One* chance, man," I said, knowing he'd decided, knowing he wasn't going to help me. "I can do it. I *will* do it. I swear."

And then the miracle.

"If I do this for you, you will come here every week and I will ask you questions and you will *never, ever* lie to me again. If you take so much as a puff, you will tell me so. If you're late for a single class, I want to know it."

"Okay," I said, and I meant it.

"I'll talk to the Crown," he said. Whatever that meant, it must have worked, because there were no more charges.

From that day on everything changed between Daniels and me. *I* owed *him*, but for some reason that made a bigger difference in how *he* treated *me* than the other way around. And, instead of doing the in and out routine, we started to talk.

First thing every appointment, he asked me the two questions he'd promised. He'd watch me like a hawk when I answered, looking for any sign that I wasn't being truthful, or that I was holding anything back.

I never lied or hid anything from him. I never had to.

We talked about other stuff, too, and sometimes he made me mad, like the time I got talking about what it was like not to have a father.

"Oh, boo-hoo," he said. "*My* old man was drunk most of the years I was growing up. He made life at our place pure hell, no two ways about it. Nothing you can do about that stuff; you've just got to get on with it."

"I wasn't *looking* for sympathy," I said hotly. "I was just saying that's how it is."

"Yeah, okay," he said. His voice got quieter. "Things aren't always easy, I know. Where *is* your old man anyway?"

"No idea. He took off when I was a kid."

"Why don't you look him up? Maybe you can find him, ask a few questions."

"Yeah, maybe," I said, but I knew I never would.

I sometimes wonder how different things would have been if Daniels hadn't helped me, and I'd ended up getting sent away somewhere.

One thing is sure, it wouldn't have been good. And none of the stuff that happened when The Watcher came along would likely have taken place at all.

chapter nine

Even though, like I said, I'd mellowed out a lot since back then, I was no pushover. And I wasn't what you'd call excited at the thought of spending my Saturdays in a stupid bakery — for zero pay.

"You know we're just going to be wasting our time," I said to Tack. "That girl *has* to have a boyfriend already. There's no way someone who looks like her is just kicking around free."

That was when he told me that he knew for a fact that she didn't — because he'd checked her out. Weirdest thing was, he'd persuaded his ex-girlfriend, Teisha Johnson, to get the information for him. If I asked someone I used to date to do something like that, all I'd get would be a slap in the mouth.

Before I could spend much time thinking about that, though, he dropped another bomb. According to

Teisha's sources, the girl, whose name was Mira, went to a private school and wasn't allowed to date.

"You mean to tell me ..."

But Tack waved off my protests. He actually insisted that once Dunja got to know him, she'd be only too happy to have her niece dating him. I thought of the aunt's unfriendly face and *knew* he was hallucinating.

Even so, just before five o'clock on Saturday morning, off we went, Tack whistling and me plodding along half asleep. I muttered a few things about how this girl was clearly going to be trouble and he was a mental case if he thought otherwise, but he just kept on smiling and whistling.

It occurred to me at one point that if *he* was crazy to be doing this just to be around this Mira person, then *I* must be even crazier than he was, to be going along for absolutely no good reason. Except, he'd do the same thing for me if things were switched around.

Like last month, at Pockets — a neighbourhood pool hall — he'd put down coin, but when his turn came up, this girl I sort of like, Lavender Dean, was on the table. He stepped off and gave me the spot without a word, which I knew he'd do.

That's a small thing, of course. I mean, it's not like he gave me a kidney or anything, but it's one of the ways you know someone is solid, when they do the right thing without even stopping to think about it.

Anyway, when we got to the bakery that morning, Mira wasn't even there. I managed to keep my mouth shut about that, but it wasn't easy.

Dunja was no joy to work for, either. She acted like we should know what to do without being told and made what I *know* were rude comments in another language when we didn't. Even Tack was losing some of his cheerfulness after a couple of hours of that.

Then Mira arrived. She smiled at us and said hello, but after tying on an apron (something which I hate to tell you, Tack and I were also wearing) she spent most of her time out front — first setting up the displays and later waiting on customers.

By twelve o'clock, which was the time Dunja had generously decided to let us — the *unpaid* help — off work, I never wanted to see flour or shortening or sugar again. And don't even get me started on eggs. I'd been given the job of separating forty of them, which is no easy thing considering how slippery they are and how easy it is for bits of shell to break off and end up in the bowl.

But I did it, and what do you think happened next? Dunja threw the yolks into this batter she was making and then, not five minutes later, she beat the whites and tossed them in too! I mean, if you're going to put them all in there anyway, why take them apart in the first place?

The worst thing was the way the place smelled. Think about it. There I was, no breakfast, stuck in a kitchen with breads and cakes and cookies and stuff all baking away. It was all I could do not to start eating my way out of bondage, like the prisoner I was.

"You'd think she could have given us some lunch," I grumbled as we headed toward our street.

"Mmm," Tack said. It was hard to tell if he'd even heard me.

Except food was suddenly unimportant, because there, on the other side of the street, was The Watcher. He was standing in front of a shoe store just a short distance ahead of us, but he was looking in our direction.

This time I decided to act like I didn't notice him, just to see what he was up to. Sure enough, as soon as we passed him he started ambling along the same way we were going, staying on the other side of the street, moving steadily enough to keep us in sight.

"Tack," I said, "don't look now but there's a guy across the street who's been following me for the last few weeks."

"Say *what*?" Tack started to look, which was exactly what I'd just told him *not* to do.

I bumped into him on purpose, throwing him off balance enough to keep him from gawking and letting the guy know I'd spotted him.

"*Don't look,*" I repeated.

"Aw, man, who'd be followin' *you*?" Tack said.

"I dunno, but I've caught him at it a few times recently," I said. "C'mon, let's speed up a bit and see if he stays with us."

We stepped it up, hurrying along until we reached our street, which was at the next corner. We turned up and went a short way. I pretended to drop something and start searching around for it. Tack joined me.

"That's him," I hissed, a jolt running through me at the sight of the guy, now heading straight toward us from around the corner.

But the guy must have realized that he was spotted. He turned off the sidewalk and headed toward the same apartment building he'd used for cover another time. Only, when he got to the security door, he made a big show of checking through his pockets and acting like he couldn't find his keys.

He pressed a buzzer — or maybe more than one — and a minute later he pulled the door open and went into the building.

"Looks like the dude lives there," Tack said.

"No, he knows we saw him and he's just covering for himself. Did you notice how he 'couldn't find' his keys and had to get someone to buzz him in?"

Tack thought I was imagining things at first but

when I explained about how I'd caught the guy watching me a couple of other times in the past week or two, he stopped scoffing.

"Who you think it could be?" he asked as we got to my apartment.

"I don't know," I said. "My father, maybe."

"Serious? You think that's your father?"

"Maybe. I don't really remember what he looks like, but this guy seems kind of familiar to me, so it could be him."

"You got no pictures of your dad? Nuthin'?"

"Mom got rid of anything like that a long time ago. All I have is a vague idea, and I know his hair is dark, like this guy's."

"Wonder what he wants," Tack mused.

"Beats me. Maybe he got curious about what I look like. And I'm only guessing about who this guy is — or could be. I just can't think of anyone else who might be following me around."

"You gonna talk to him?"

I shrugged. All of a sudden I wished I hadn't mentioned the guy to Tack at all. I changed the subject, which was as easy as mentioning Mira.

While Tack got animated discussing his big plans to win over the girl and her aunt, I let my mind drift. I realized that if I was going to find out who The

Watcher was and why he was following me, I was going to have to come up with a plan.

The idea to give him the slip and start following him hit me almost immediately. I turned it over in my head, knowing it wouldn't be quite as simple as it sounded. I'd have to fine tune the details if I was going to make it work.

In the meantime, there were other things going on. It seemed the patch job on Lynn's relationship with Conor hadn't quite done the trick. When I got back to the apartment she was there again, only this time she had a battered old suitcase and a couple of bulging trash bags with her.

chapter ten

"Where's Mom?" Lynn asked sullenly as soon as I came through the door. Her eyes were red-rimmed, but at least she wasn't crying at that moment.

"Where is she usually?" I said. "She's somewhere in the building smoking and drinking coffee, talking about how the government should be giving single mothers more money to live on, or what a loser the last guy she dated was, or which reality show she likes the best."

Lynn almost smiled. "Yeah, that sounds about right. Did she say anything about cooking today?"

"I wasn't talking to her this morning. She was still sleeping when I left." I almost told her about the bakery thing, but stopped myself.

"Yeah, well, I gotta talk to her. I need to stay here for a while." She looked at me pointedly, like she was waiting for me to offer her my room. As if.

Actually, this same scene had already played out about six, eight months ago, and it had turned into a big pain for me. Mom and Lynn had both gone on and on about how girls need privacy more than boys do. They couldn't explain *why*, exactly, but they kept at the theme with true female persistence, giving "reasons" that amounted to nothing. Like, Mom kept saying, "because she's a girl, that's why," with her hands on her hips until I thought I might flip out completely.

After what seemed like a three day long, non-stop argument, I'd given in — just to shut them up. This time, it wasn't happening.

Still, I knew from experience that they could wear me down if they were really determined. I figured a pre-emptive strike was in order. I waited for about an hour, then plunked down on the couch beside Lynn, who was drowning her sorrows in a stupid soap opera.

"Uh, do you know anything about...?" I let my words trail off deliberately. She can't stand that and I knew she'd practically torture me, if she had to, in order to get me to finish what I'd started saying.

"What? Do I know anything about what?"

"Nothing. Forget it."

"Porter, you tell me what you were going to say *right now!*" She tilted her head sharply and put on what she probably considered a fierce face.

I almost laughed at that. What was she going to do, overpower me with her massive five-foot-three, hundred-and-five-pound physique? She's tried that a few times over the past years, when she's been especially outraged over some "terrible thing" I've done. And let me tell you, it doesn't take much for her to see a thing as terrible.

Anyway, she'd come at me when that happened — arms flailing and (I swear) eyes closed. Nuttiest sight you ever saw. She was no more threatening than a housefly and about as much of a challenge to swat away. Not that I actually swatted her. I'd just get hold of her wrists and stand back until she wore herself out trying to kick me. Then I'd kind of walk her to a chair and plop her down.

This was no time for any of that, though, not if I was going to save my room. I pushed those thoughts off and kept a serious look on my face. Then I let her slowly coax it out of me, but not until I'd made her swear she wouldn't tell anyone because it was embarrassing. I thought that was a nice touch — kind of made it sound more realistic, in case she wasn't entirely convinced.

"Okay, okay," I said at last. "Do you know anything about fungus?"

"Fungus?" she said, in a tone that was so disgusted you'd have thought I'd offered her some for dinner.

"Yeah, like, in a rash ... on a person."

She looked horrified. "Whereabouts?" she asked, leaning away from me.

"Uh, it's kind of a travelling condition," I said, barely managing to hang onto my straight face. "It seems to move around. First it's in one place, then that clears and it shows up somewhere else."

"Eeeww."

"Yeah, I know. It's real itchy, too." I scratched a couple of spots on my legs and chest for good measure. "And scaly. Want to feel it?"

"No!" she nearly shrieked before getting a hold of herself. "I don't want to be mean or anything, but it could be contagious. You should see a doctor right away."

"I dunno, it'll probably clear up eventually," I said. "I've only had it for a few months."

"Porter! You have to see a doctor! Does Mom know about it?"

I shook my head sadly. "You're the only person I felt like I could talk to." I thought that was a nice touch. Lynn's face softened.

"I'm so glad you felt you could come to me," she said, almost choking up. "But you *have* to see a doctor!"

"Okay, okay," I said. "Just don't tell Mom."

"I won't, if you *promise* to get it looked at right away."

"I will" I said solemnly. "I'll go to the walk-in clinic tomorrow, right after school."

I don't want you to get the idea from this that I'm one of those casual liars who'd rather make something up than tell the truth. I'm not. I'm no saint, but I'm usually pretty truthful. This, however, was an emergency situation and I preferred to think of the story as more of a trick than an actual lie. Anyway, when Mom came home a couple of hours later I didn't think I was going to have to worry about a big fight over my room. I was right.

First Mom raved about Lynn's situation, going on about how she'd *always* said Conor was no good (she'd never said that) and how Lynn should be dating a doctor or lawyer (she must think doctors and lawyers are just dying to date high school dropouts) and of course she can stay with us as long as she needs to and Porter will be glad to let her use his room again.

I didn't even have to open my mouth.

"Uh, no, that's okay," Lynn smiled, trying to act like she was being fair. "He let me have it last time. I don't want to kick him out of his own room again."

"Don't be silly." Mom waved a hand as she spoke. "You're a girl. Girls need more privacy than boys."

"No, it's *okay*," Lynn repeated. She looked at me uneasily, like even the mention of using my room might cause fungus to start growing on her. "I'd *rather* sleep out here."

They went around it a couple of times, which was entertaining for me, since I had no part in the argument. In the end, Lynn persuaded Mom that she wanted to be able to watch TV to help her fall asleep and the whole thing was dropped.

"Did you kids eat?" Mom thought to ask then. "I can fry some eggs and wieners for you."

"That'd be great," I said quickly, before Lynn could tell her we'd had some Kraft dinner a while earlier. I can *always* eat.

"I don't know, maybe one egg for me," Lynn decided. "I'm too upset to be able to eat much." That was true. She'd picked at her bowl of KD and almost half of it had gone into the garbage.

Mom fussed over her as she cooked. She went on about how the whole thing was a blessing in disguise because it would give Lynn a chance to get back on her own two feet.

"You've got to keep your strength up," Mom told her (for what, I couldn't tell you — Lynn hadn't worked in six months or more).

"I will, Mom," Lynn said, sniffling.

Mom nodded. "Well, eat your egg, dear. Remember that time heals all wounds." (How that tied into eating an egg, I had no idea.)

There was no mention of Lynn getting a job, which you'd think would be on the top of the list for someone who was supposed to be getting back on her own two feet. Maybe that was because Mom hadn't worked in so many years herself. I used to wish she'd get a job, spend some time in the real world, or barring that, that she'd put a little more effort into taking care of our place. The apartment gets pretty grungy sometimes and even the laundry builds up until I lug it down to the washers in the basement.

I think maybe she was depressed and couldn't drag herself out of the slump. When she wasn't at someone else's place she slept a lot, right in the middle of the day and everything. Maybe it was a way of escaping her own life.

Tack's mother wasn't anything like mine. She kept her place spotless, but she also ruled her boys like a drill sergeant, and she always had something critical to say to them. It seemed like she didn't even like her own kids, the way she was always telling them they were lazy and stupid and wouldn't amount to anything. Like your father, she'd say. She slapped them sometimes, too, right across the side of the head.

I found it weird how they just all took it. Not one of them talked back, or tried to stop her from hitting them when she went that far.

My mother did slam me up against the wall once, when I was younger. We were having a fight about something — I don't remember what — and all of a sudden she just grabbed me and pushed me, with my T-shirt clumped in her fist.

Then she kind of hissed at me, which is the best way I can describe it, and told me *she* was the boss, and as long as I was living in *her* house, I'd follow *her* rules. I was so mad I wanted to punch her right in the face, but she was acting like something possessed, which scared me, too, so I backed down. I guess she thought she won something that day.

Of course, that was a long time ago and there have been some changes since then.

chapter eleven

I wasn't crazy about having Lynn around again — not full-time anyway — but I have to admit there *were* some good things about it. The big one was that she liked to cook. She was also a way better housekeeper than Mom. It was almost like cooking and cleaning were her twisted little way of rebelling — and not being like her mother.

Even when Lynn would just drop by to visit, she'd almost always wash a floor or scrub the bathroom or something. She'd tell me useful stuff, too, like how to get a stain out of a shirt or how to cook things right. I never used to cook meat even if there was some in the freezer, because it always turned out dry and tough as leather. But, thanks to Lynn, I learned to do a fairly decent job cooking most basic things.

On the other hand, she liked to talk. Not normal conversations, which might have been all right, but relationship stuff, like how guys and girls feel and think differently and stuff. It's all idiotic if you ask me. I used to think if she said one more "meaningful" thing to me, I was going to lose it completely.

I didn't think it would last long, though, so I tried to be patient and put up with her, especially since I heard her crying quietly to herself a few times. Even so, I had to fight the urge to flee whenever she got that certain look on her face and asked me if we could talk.

I've learned from experience that when a female — and it doesn't matter if it's your sister or mother or girl-friend, it's all the same — says "We need to talk," what she *really* means is "let's discuss your shortcomings," or, in a slight variation, "let's discuss the shortcomings of all males." Lynn wasn't complaining about me, exactly. I was more a stand-in for Conor (he's actually a good guy and I never understood what he saw in my sister) and kind of a representative for males in general.

Her rants got really tiresome after about five minutes and she could go on for hours, mostly repeating herself in what I'm sure she thought were new and insightful ways. I didn't totally avoid her, but I admit I spent more time than usual at Tack's place, or just kicking around.

After the first few days it looked like maybe she really wasn't going back with Conor. He called a couple of times and even came over once, but they just ended up fighting. By the next weekend I'd resigned myself to the idea that she'd be around for a while. Still, I kept hoping that they'd put it back together eventually. Until Saturday, that is.

Tack was on his way over, so when there was a knock at the door, I just hollered "c'mon in" like usual. The door opened and this dude stepped in, only it wasn't Tack or anyone else I knew.

I thought he had the wrong place but then Lynn came hurrying along from down the hall and went up to him with a big smile and kissed him. It was just on the cheek but it still shocked me to see it. I mean, she'd been with Conor since she was barely seventeen. How could she be about to go out on a date with this other guy so soon after they split? In fact, when did she even have time to *meet* someone else?

"Oh," she said, seeing me staring at them, "this is my brother, Porter." She sounded like she was apologizing. "And, this is Daryl."

"Hey! How ya doing?" he said. He gave a slow, one-motion wave, like a salute in the middle of the air. Probably thought it was cool. Made him look like an idiot.

"Yeah, hi," I mumbled and turned back toward the TV.

Tack arrived just then and Lynn launched into another introduction. Tack was a little friendlier than I'd been, though he seemed puzzled.

"Well, we're off," Lynn said cheerfully, like she wasn't doing a single thing wrong.

"Great meeting you guys," Daryl added.

I ignored him and asked Lynn what she wanted me to tell her boyfriend if he called.

"I don't *have* a boyfriend," she said, but her voice wavered just a bit.

"Who was that?" Tack asked me as soon as they'd left.

"I don't know or care," I said.

"Uh-huh." He dropped it. "So, you ready to go?"

We'd made plans to hang out at Pockets. It was kind of a fallback for us when we had nothing else to do because it was cheap. Two bucks a game if you were playing but you could just hang out and watch if you wanted.

Tack and I were both average players, so whether or not we shot a game depended on who was around. Some girls were impressed if you had a cool attitude and a cue in your hand. But a few were slick and accurate on the felt themselves and you didn't want to be shooting in front of them.

Tubby, the owner (who was actually frightfully thin) was an all right guy. He had rules and stuff but they were fair, and he only charged a buck for fountain pop.

We checked our funds and found that between us we had a little over seven dollars. Most of it was Tack's — he earned a bit here and there by doing odd jobs for a few people in his building. I usually found a way to pick up a few bucks, too, cleaning cars mostly, but there hadn't been much going on that week.

Didn't matter. We always threw in together. It evened out in the long run.

So, we were walking along and I was drifting a bit, thinking about this and that, when Tack alerted me to the fact that The Watcher was coming up behind us. I tried to catch a glimpse of him in a store window but in the dark with all the lights on inside and out, the reflection was too hazy.

"Take a right at the corner," I whispered to Tack.

We did, and walked half a block out of our way before turning back. The guy had disappeared.

"He must have realized we were on to him," I said, disappointed. I'd envisioned walking a ways down the street and then doing an about-face and going back like we'd forgotten something or changed our minds or whatever. In that case, The Watcher would have had no choice but to keep going, and giving him the slip would have been a cinch.

I'd thought that would be good practice for when I put my plan into place and turned things around — started watching him instead. Before I could get behind him, I'd need to figure out a few ways to throw him off when he was following me.

I figured Tack had done something that tipped him off this time. No big deal. It would be easier when I was on my own.

I'd been thinking about it a lot and I was just about ready to get started. In the meantime, the pool hall waited, and I had a particular reason for wanting to get there.

chapter twelve

It looked like Tack and I might finally make it to Pockets after our detour, though we'd had another "offer" on the way when we ran into a couple of guys from school — Jake and Lee. They were heading to a party at Tiffany Rutledge's place and they stopped to ask if we wanted to crash it.

"She's like, unveiling her new piercing tonight," Lee said. He looked like he might hang out his tongue and start panting any second. I didn't personally have much interest in finding out what part of her body Tiffany had decided to stick a hole in this time. Besides, Lavender Dean was supposed to be at Pockets and running into her was hardly ever the worst thing in the world.

We told them thanks but we already had plans.

"Cool," Lee said. He grinned like we were sharing a joke.

"You got any smoke, man?" Jake asked unsteadily. By the look of them they'd already been into something a lot stronger than weed, but these two never seem to think they're high enough.

We told them we didn't and they left, making their way along the street in stumbles and lurches, which amused them to no end. I wondered, if it hadn't been for Daniels, whether I'd be in the same shape they were. It wasn't all that long ago that I made a regular habit of spending evenings floating along with that half-disembodied feeling.

No denying it — the pull is still there at times. The old urge to disconnect. It had seemed like a kind of freedom, except *that* had turned out to be an illusion.

I never saw it that way until I got probation — and Daniels. There were so many things that changed for me that year. It used to get to me, the way he seemed to see things. He was forever making casual observations, only they were almost always dead-on. It was as if he could see right into my brain.

"You think anything you've gone through is unique?" he asked once. "Like no one else has ever lain on their bed and fought for breath over the crushing weight on their chest? You think it's anger or hurt or something else, but what it *really* is, is *want*. All the stuff that fate hasn't given you. What swells up in a person that way is hardly ever what *is*, but what *isn't*. We can deal with the garbage that gets dumped on us — we learn how to handle that. But we never learn to stop wanting the things that are missing."

"Did you feel that way when you were my age?" I asked, sure he'd tell me we weren't there to talk about him.

"Yeah, sure," he said, surprising me. "Like I said, you can get used to almost anything. So if your father comes in falling down drunk, roaring and breaking things in the middle of the night, you find ways to get through it. What's harder to deal with — or forgive — are the things that just aren't there. Someone to help you lace up your skates, shoot some hoops, teach you to skip rocks, go camping. All the everyday stuff."

Later on, when we'd moved past that and got to the place where we could really talk — and probably when I was more ready to hear him — *then* he seemed to mostly listen.

He was different. When I first met him I'd thought he was just a lazy slacker who couldn't be bothered to do his job. Truth was, he was tuned in enough to know what to say and when. Mostly, he *heard* more than any other adult I've ever known.

In my experience, most of the time, no one's listening or paying attention — not enough to hear any of the stuff that really matters. It's like most people won't look too close in case they find out something they don't like, because that might disturb the nice order of things.

Like the year that Krystal Smithton OD'd on smack. She was with some friends, and word on the street was they took care of a few things before calling 911 — as if the emergency people were going to stop and search the place.

There were a few stories about what happened, but whatever the truth was, Krystal didn't make it. Maybe she would have if they'd called right away and maybe it was already too late for her by the time anyone noticed she wasn't just spaced out.

The really pathetic thing was how her parents blamed everyone else. Even after they'd been shown all the track marks, they refused to believe she'd been a druggie. They hung on to the idea that she'd been peer-pressured into using, and talked about her death like it was a murder.

I hadn't known Krystal, except from school, but I knew she'd been a stoner since around grade six — and that she'd moved up quickly from weed and had made her way to heroin the year before she died. Word was that she'd done whatever she had to do to make sure she could fix, and she'd been beaten up a couple of times although I don't know the details. So, how could it have been that her own parents *hadn't known* she was a doper? I'd have known within two minutes if I'd just met her for the first time.

My mother would never have missed all of the signs Krystal's folks missed. But back when I was smoking bud, she never once noticed anything different. Or, if she did, she never brought it up, and I think she would have if she'd realized. Come to think of it, we never talked about drugs — not *really.*

Oh, she gave me the speech once. Drugs are bad. Drugs will hurt you. Only losers use drugs. It was like having someone read to me from a grade one lesson book. "See kids use drugs. See kids drop out of school. Don't, kids, don't!"

Tack's mother had a different approach. Her approach with him was: "I ever catch you using drugs and I will kick your sorry butt all over the city of Toronto and back." Tack could do a wicked imitation of that when he was stoned. We'd laugh ourselves sick.

But Daniels knew the score. He talked to me on a level playing field, too, once I'd cleaned up. Lots of times I found myself saying things I hadn't even known were in my head and some of them were pretty weird. Surprisingly, when we were talking, no matter what I told him, he never acted like the big P.O., if you know what I mean. And that made me tell him more — almost like I was trying to force him to react, to show his disapproval, to judge me. Only, he never did.

One day I found myself telling him the whole story about the bong.

"So this bong," he said, "what was it that made you want it so much?"

"Uh, it looked ..." I hesitated, half embarrassed. "I know this sounds stupid, but it looked wise."

"Like it had answers?"

"Yeah, I guess." Feeling stupid, I added, "It's not like I asked it questions or anything."

"But you *have* questions."

"Sure. Doesn't everyone?"

"I guess they do. Say you could ask the bong *one* thing and it would answer you, what would you ask?"

I laughed and shook my head. "I dunno, man. That's hard to say."

"Because you can't pick the *right* question or because there are *too many?*"

"Probably both." I noticed that Daniels had drifted, and could see that he was thinking about what he'd just asked me.

"What about you," I said. "What would you ask?"

He seemed to think it over, and I thought something flashed across his eyes, like he'd decided, but then he just turned his hands palms up and shrugged.

"You're right," he said. "That's a tough one."

Other times we just talked about school and sports and general stuff. Then, one day, when we were wrapping things up, he said, "So, I guess you've probably done the math. But in case you haven't, this is it. Your year is up. This is our last appointment."

"I'm not on probation anymore?" My mouth had a hard time getting around the words.

"Nope." He stretched a hand out. "You did all right, kid."

I shook his hand and squared my jaw. "Well, it wasn't so bad."

"You have my number. Feel free to call if you run into any problems I can help with," he said. "Otherwise, good luck and all that. You're going to do okay … you know that, don't you?"

"Yeah, thanks." I stood up.

"Oh, there's one more thing." He reached down beside him and picked up a book. He passed it across the desk.

"This is for you."

I looked at the book. I read the title out loud. "*A Prayer for Owen Meany.*"

"It's my favourite John Irving novel," he said. "I thought you might like it."

I held it up like I was showing it to him. "I'll definitely read it. Thanks."

"Yeah, no problem."

We said "So, all right then" and "Take care," and a couple of things like that — the words you say when you can't say the real stuff.

Then I left his office for the last time.

All the way home I kept looking at the book, glancing down to where it was tucked between my arm and chest. It was — believe it or not — the first time anyone had ever given me a book.

The front cover displayed a picture of one of those things for making women's clothes. I read the back cover and wasn't sure I'd much like the story. It didn't sound very exciting.

But I knew I'd read it right away.

chapter thirteen

Strains of the latest Nickleback CD met us before we reached the door at Pockets. Tubby played mostly Canadian groups and tunes — a pretty decent mix of new stuff and the classics. Lately he'd been playing a lot of Nickleback, Roman Dane, and old Bryan Adams.

We ambled over to where Tubby was sitting and said hello to him.

"Hey, how are you guys tonight?" He reached under the counter, pulled out a package of Nicorette gum and popped a piece into his mouth. Tubby quits smoking about once a month.

"Good. You?"

"Can't complain." He chewed vigorously, not like they show on TV — bite, bite, stop. "And no one would listen if I did."

That didn't call for an answer, so we ordered a couple of Pepsis and then sauntered over to the tables.

They were all occupied. We plunked down on a long bench along the right wall. I tried to see if Lavender was around, without making it obvious that I was looking.

"Think we should put up for a game?" Tack asked.

I'd made a point of looking over the players at each table, which was also a good way to see who was around without seeming to. The place was busier than usual but I didn't see Lavender anywhere.

"I dunno. They've all got two or three holds now," I said.

What you did was put a toonie down behind the last one in line to reserve whichever table you wanted. When your turn came up, you put your toonie into the side slot to release the balls, then racked 'em up.

Without knowing who had reserved the tables or in what order, it was hard to know which table to hold.

We always dropped two toonies on one table and then Tack would take the first game because he was a better player than I was. We'd pick a table that didn't have strong players lined up, to more or less guarantee that he'd win his game. Then I'd be up next to play him.

Of course, it didn't always work out. Sometimes he would lose and I'd end up playing someone else. No big deal; that was just the way it went. All you could do was try to arrange things the way you wanted them and then live with whatever happened.

"I dunno," I said. "It'll be a while before there's a table free. What do you think?"

We talked it over and decided to hang around for a bit, anyway. Since we could always pick up our money and leave if we wanted to, we dropped our coins on the back table and then wandered around to check things out.

Loren Vasey was shooting at the centre table and we stopped to watch her for a few minutes, admiring the smooth movements that sent the balls into one pocket after another. She had a good eye and steady hand and could beat almost anyone. We hadn't even hesitated before passing up that table when we were deciding where to place our money. She'd most likely be around until closing and, unless she decided to take a break, anyone lined up for that table was pretty well guaranteed to play her. And lose.

Loren and I had never been friends, really, so I was surprised when she spoke to me. If you'd asked me if she even knew I was there, I'd have said no way.

"Hey, Porter."

"Hey."

"I've never played you, have I?"

Ah. So she was looking for a fresh victim. Probably tired of beating the same guys over and over.

"I don't think so," I said, like I wasn't sure.

"So, how about it?" She flashed me a smile and then turned back to the table to point out a combination shot that I couldn't make if I had a hundred chances. She chalked up, leaned over the table, and slid her cue forward just once to line up the shot before making it. She turned back to me without even watching to see if it all happened as she'd predicted, which, of course, it did.

"Uh, I already put up at another table," I said. It sounded pretty lame.

"Which one?"

I pointed to the back of the room. At the same time, I felt Tack nudge me in the back with his elbow. It was a *What are you, nuts? Go for it!* kind of nudge. I almost lost my balance. Terrific.

"So, I'll put up for a game with you at this table," she said, plopping down a toonie. "You can play at whichever one is free first."

But there was no question as to which one would be free first — not the way she shot — and she knew it as well as I did. She could wrap the table in a quarter of the time it normally took to play.

"Yeah, okay. Sure." I tried to look enthusiastic while I prepared myself for the coming humiliation.

I made my way back to the corner and parked myself on the bench, wondering if there was any way to get out of playing her.

"*What* is your *prob*lem, dude?" Tack asked.

"What, you mean because I'm not dying to look like a fool?"

"C'mon, man, who cares? She's *hot*."

"She just wants a fresh sacrifice," I pointed out.

"Maybe," he said. "Could be more to it."

"Sure, because she's always going out with guys just like me," I said.

He didn't have an answer for that. We both knew Loren wasn't about to start hanging out with anyone my age, and especially not someone who was always broke. Her taste ran to older guys with cars, guys who all had a certain look about them — like they were always on the verge of sneering. At everything.

Tack was, as usual, being the optimist, thinking she could have more on her mind than the desire to add another idiot to the long line of guys she'd embarrassed at the pool table. But it turned out he was right, just not for the reason he thought.

She beat the players who had already lined up at her table in no time and then signalled me that I was up. I walked over, wondering if my fake smile was fooling her.

"You still on probation?" she asked as I racked the balls and stepped back to let her break.

"Don't waste any time getting to the point," I said. But I smiled, because it really didn't bother me. I like girls who are direct a lot more than the ones who put on a big coy act while they work their way up to whatever they really want to say.

"We probably don't *have* much time," she said, smiling back. "I've *seen* you play."

She chalked up and broke. She got low, and her eyes swept the table, assessing which shot she should take next. You can always tell the good players because they never go for the easy shots first.

"So, are you?" she said.

"Seeing as you paid good money to get this information," I said, "the answer is no, I'm not."

"But you were?"

"Until last year, yeah. Why?"

"I just wanted to know how things work. I had to hold, you know, for Jack."

"What's the charge?" I guessed Jack was the current boyfriend. A real winner by the sounds of it. You just can't help admire a guy who expects his girlfriend to take a fall for him.

"I dunno. They didn't tell me that yet. But it was mostly just weed."

"How much?"

"Half an ounce, maybe. And some E, but just five."

"I don't know. It's probably going to be trafficking. Is this your first charge?"

She nodded before lifting her chin and asking, "So, what should I expect?"

"I honestly have no idea. Sorry."

Loren shrugged like it didn't matter, then leaned forward and sank two more balls in quick succession. She stepped back after the second.

"I didn't call that one off the rail," she said, nodding for me to go ahead.

"Oh, right." I chalked my cue and looked the table over, hoping for an easy shot. The five was sitting in a nice line with a corner. I dropped it straight in no problem and then went for the one.

I glanced up from my second shot, which I'd miraculously made, and was startled to see Lavender Dean standing a few metres away, watching. She gave me a hesitant wave. I smiled at her, hoping she'd seen my two good shots. A sudden rise in my pulse made it unlikely I'd manage a third. I didn't.

"If you happen to get a P.O. named Andrew Daniels, let me know," I told Loren. "I'd give him a call, put in a word for you or whatever."

"Yeah, okay. Thanks." Loren sank her last three balls and then shot hard at the eight, which was barely in front of a corner pocket. My single hope that she might scratch on it died when the cue ball stopped dead, just a hair from the pocket.

I told her good game and tried to look casual as I walked over to where Lavender stood.

"Hey," I said.

"Hey." She looked good, kind of glowing.

I tried to think of something cool to say. I came up with, "So, you just get here?"

"A few minutes ago. You?"

"Been here a little while." How could she *resist* that kind of witty repartee?

"Mmm." She smiled again and then looked down, kind of shy. Made me want to pull her over and hold her against me.

The thing about Lavender was that she was hard to read. She was always friendly to me, which might have meant something except she was basically that way toward everyone.

Sometimes it seemed as though she really liked me, but other times I wasn't so sure. I'd been kind of toying with the idea of asking her out for a few months but I couldn't seem to work up to it. It wasn't like I hadn't been shot down before, but with her, it mattered more. I knew if she said no, that'd be it.

I figured there was no sense rushing into anything.

chapter fourteen

I woke up that Saturday morning to the sound of banging, followed by Lynn yelling my name from the living room.

Struggling to pull myself awake, I was halfway down the hall before I realized that what I was hearing was someone knocking at the door.

"Where are my shoes?" I mumbled, though why that particular question had fought its way to the surface of my brain, I have no idea.

"Yo, Porter. Open up, man!"

"Tack?" I said, yanking open the door. "*What* are you doing here so early?"

"Your brain fogged or what?" he shook his head. "We gotta get to the bakery."

"I'm not even up," I groaned.

"No kiddin'."

"Would you guys *shut up!*" Lynn sounded a bit testy. I wondered what time she'd finally wandered in the night before. The couch she was sleeping on had been unoccupied when I'd gotten home, and that was around one o'clock.

"I gotta shower," I said as the haze lifted. "Give me ten minutes."

A hot shower finished waking me and I threw on some clothes and mechanically towelled my hair dry while I gulped down a bowl of Shreddies.

"You are *so* disgusting," Lynn said. "How can you dry your hair like that while you're eating?"

I knew what she meant, but I said, "Why? I've got two hands." She called me a pig and then turned to the back of the couch and flung the comforter up over her head.

"*What* is going on out here?"

None of us had heard Mom coming and her sudden appearance at the end of the hall brought instant silence. If there was one thing Mom didn't like, it was being woken up. That's why I hardly ever saw her in the mornings.

Of course, I didn't see her much in the daytime either, unless she decided to cook supper, which wasn't often. Otherwise, she'd wander in and flop in front of the TV or head straight to bed sometime late in the evening, after she'd exhausted the coffee rounds.

"Sorry," I said. "We'll be quiet."

For some reason, it hit me right then that quiet already filled most of the time we spent in the same room. I wondered how long it had been since she'd said more than a dozen words to me in a day. Seemed like a long time since I'd heard anything other than "Got your homework done?" or "You eat yet?" or other automatic questions.

"I'd better not hear another sound," she said. Then she turned and shuffled back to her room. Her bare feet hardly lifted off the floor. I had a sudden, angry urge to yell at her, to say something that would start a big fight.

I said nothing, though. All that would get me would be some yelling and threats that she could send me to live in a detention centre, or worse, with my father, and then I could see what it was like to have it rough and that maybe after a few months of that I'd appreciate her and everything she'd sacrificed for me.

Once, when I was about twelve, I'd gotten so angry during an argument that I'd said, "So go ahead! Send me to live with my father then!" It hadn't been a particularly smart thing to say. She'd grabbed me by the shirt and screamed in my face, and the next thing I knew I was standing out in the hallway with the door locked behind me.

I was there for hours. At first I knocked and then I called out a few things like I was sorry and stuff, but after a while I just stayed quiet and waited because people down the hall were opening their doors and looking out at me.

By the time she let me in I had to pee so bad that I almost couldn't hold it until I got to the bathroom. I guess I could have gone somewhere else, even though I just had socks on, but I was too afraid to leave. I was sure that if she opened the door and I wasn't there, she'd make me spend the night in the hall.

In the bathroom, relief made my knees shake as I stood in front of the toilet and peed. And cried. That's not the coolest thing to admit to, but I'm telling the truth here and I guess that means all of it.

That's not the only fight we'd had where she made me understand that *she had all the power.* I learned not to challenge her, not to argue, not to expect any kind of voice in decisions that affected me. By the time I was sixteen, our lives were so separate there really wasn't anything much to fight over.

I just kept her off my case as much as I could and didn't stir things up. Made life easier for me.

I thought about this as Tack and I walked toward the bakery. And I thought about The Watcher and wondered, if he *was* my father, what my mom would say or do if she found out he was around.

I wasn't about to mention anything about it to her, that's for sure.

The last time I'd seen him I'd been four years old. I hadn't thought about that in a long time. Back then we were living in a basement apartment; I don't know what part of the city it was in. Lynn was in school and I went to daycare somewhere within walking distance of our place.

I can't say whether Mom was dropping me off or picking me up the day he showed up there. Either way, I know I never went back to that daycare, and we moved not long afterward. Mom said it wasn't safe.

I still remember how she screamed that day, and how I turned automatically to see what had frightened her like that.

He was standing across the street, just looking at me. His hand floated out, reaching — like he was offering something. An urge to run to him rose and drained away in a flash.

Then I was scared. Terrified in fact. Fear choked me, like it had wrapped itself around my throat. Mom started yelling then, and cascades of anger and hatred spilled with her words, which ended with, "The kids *hate* you, do you hear me! They *hate* you."

Then her instruction to me, to tell him. Do it. Tell him *right now*.

"I hate you," I'd said when I could get my voice to work. My face was wet. Everything had turned into freeze frames.

His hand went up, lit on his mouth for a second and then tilted forward. He blew a kiss at me. His face contorted. He turned away.

"If he ever comes near you," my mother told me as she pushed me along the sidewalk, "if you *ever* see him *anywhere*, you run. Run as fast as you can."

That was the theme of my childhood.

I thought it odd that The Watcher's presence, if indeed he was my father, didn't seem to frighten me.

Maybe that was because my memories were as thin and hazy as a cold grey dawn. Mom had filled in a lot of the blanks for me. Eventually, the things she'd told me almost seemed like memories. I used to think they were, except they lacked something, like a movie that was missing the background noises.

I'd stopped trying to work my memories to the surface a long time before. It didn't matter. Or, it hadn't.

Now, if he was back, if he was coming around, he might as well know things had changed. For one thing, I was no longer a scared little kid and I wasn't going to run.

I found myself looking for him even though it was probably way too early in the morning for him to be out following me. It was really starting to get to me, wondering what he wanted — why he'd shown up after all these years.

By the time I ran through all this stuff in my head we'd reached the bakery. As we went through the doorway I made up my mind that the next time I saw this guy on the street, I was going to try to give him the slip and follow *him*.

It was time I found out who he was for sure, and what he was up to.

chapter fifteen

"I've had it with this bakery stuff," I told Tack on the way home later. "It's a waste of time and I'm not getting up at the crack of dawn again for no good reason."

He didn't say anything and at first I thought he was mad, but then he whacked me on the arm and started laughing.

"You gone off your head, or what?" I asked, smiling in spite of myself at the way he was grinning.

"Naw, man, I'm good. I asked the aunt today 'bout the job situation and she told me she won't know for maybe three, four more weeks."

"No way."

"Yeah. I said in that case we be done today."

"Yeah? Well, *good*." A twinge of guilt hit me, and I added, "So, are you gonna forget about this girl?"

"Looks like."

It was totally out of character for Tack to give up on a girl like that and it made me immediately suspicious.

"Okay, what's going on?" I asked. "You *didn't* just decide not to bother with her."

That's when he admitted that he'd been talking to Teisha at Pockets the evening before (while I was getting my butt whipped by Loren) and that they'd decided to hook up again.

"So *why* did we go to the bakery today?" I demanded.

"*You* went 'cuz you didn't *have* this here new information. *I* went 'cuz I *said* I'd be goin'."

I let that sink in for a minute.

"You *will* pay for this," I said finally, keeping my voice calm and even. "You know that, don't you?"

"Sure do," he said.

"Just when you think it's safe — when it looks like I've forgotten all about this, revenge will come swooping down on you."

"Uh-huh," he agreed.

"I hate to see you going around nervous all the time —" I began, but then I was distracted by a familiar figure in the distance.

"I think that's him," I whispered (even though there was no way he could have heard me from that distance). "The guy who's been following me."

"You sure?" Tack squinted and peered toward the guy.

"Not a hundred percent," I admitted, "but I *think* it's him."

I had an idea then, to stop at Suleiman's — the restaurant he'd been watching me from a week or two back. It would be a good vantage point for us. Besides, I'd discovered a few bucks stashed in my dresser when I'd been fumbling for clothes earlier, and I was hungry.

By the time we got to the restaurant there was no sign of the guy, but we settled into a table where we had a view of both streets. We slouched down a bit so it wouldn't be easy for him to spot us.

Suleiman's was the main place we went to eat when we had a little coin to spend on not-so-fine dining. The place had a certain character to it that you might call charming if you weren't real fussy how you used the word.

There were eight square tables and a counter, all pretty typical of your small family-run restaurant. Some effort had been made to decorate but it didn't quite come together the way it was probably supposed to. Still, it was comfortable and familiar and we liked the feel of the place.

We stuck to the cheaper things on the menu, like hummus with warm pita bread or falafel sandwiches.

Suleiman, whom everyone called Sam, was both cook and owner. He came out of the kitchen now and then and stood at the counter, looking around and wiping his hands on his apron. When he spotted us, he always came over and shook hands and said something like "Good to see you gentlemen again," or "I hope you're finding everything satisfactory." We always told him it was the best food anywhere.

This might've even been true, for all we knew.

There was no handshake from Sam that day, since he was at the back table drinking espresso with a big bearded fellow. He lifted a hand and nodded to us like we were important customers, then he went back to what seemed like an intense discussion.

There was only one other table occupied at the time and the couple seated there was almost finished eating. The waitresses were wiping down display cases where they kept their desserts — stuff like baklava. (Lynn and I tried that once, the stacks of thin phyllo pastry layered with nuts and dripping in sticky syrup. Lynn thought it was the best thing ever but I felt like I'd been given a sugar overdose.)

Sabra, a niece of Sam's, came over to our table carrying iced water with lemon.

"You guys gonna have the usual?" she asked. She'd waited on us lots of times over the years. She also flirted with us in a kind of nervous way. I was never sure if the nervous part was because she worried that her uncle would catch her or that we'd take her seriously.

"Just hummus," I said. "No falafel."

"Special today is stuffed vine leaves," she said. "Very good."

"Nah. We got a bit of a cash flow problem." Tack sighed.

But when she came back with our order, she'd plopped a couple of the vine leaves on the edge of the plate, anyway.

"You try for the next time."

"Thanks," I said. "By the way, Sabra, there was a guy in here, oh, about a week ago, and I don't know if he ordered anything, but he stood over there for a while, staring out the window."

"I think I know the guy you mean," the other waitress, Helen, said from behind the counter. Helen was probably older than my mom but she acted a lot younger. She wore a lot of rings and makeup and she was real friendly. "He came in to use the washroom but, afterward, he didn't leave right away. Like you said, he stood by the window and looked out for a few minutes. I thought it was a bit strange. He could have seen a lot more if he'd just gone outside."

"You ever see him before, or since?" I asked, though I don't know what I was hoping to find out.

"Not that I remember," she said. "Why? Who is he?"

"I don't know," I said. I realized that if I started talking about someone following me, I'd come across as a bit whacko. "I, uh, thought he looked familiar, so I was wondering if I knew him."

That seemed to satisfy her and she told me she'd try to find out who he was if he came in again.

Tack and I took our time eating, all the while keeping our eyes peeled for any sign of The Watcher. No luck, though, and after nearly an hour we gave up and left.

I didn't ask Tack to come up when I got to my place, because it had occurred to me that maybe Lynn could tell me something. She'd been older — seven years to my four — when he and Mom had split up.

Only, Lynn wasn't home when I got to the apartment. I'd normally have seen that as a good thing since I was so used to having the place to myself. It'd been weird lately, to walk in the door and find Lynn sprawled across the couch, or painting her nails at the kitchen table, or whatever.

I made a grilled cheese sandwich and ate it while flipping through the channels to see what was on TV. After that, I ate a couple of dill pickles and wondered what Lavender was doing right then. I told myself maybe I should give her a call, just real casual, have a yak. It never got past a thought.

I'm not sure what time I fell asleep but I woke up hours later feeling disoriented and groggy. The TV was still on and I heard someone talking from what seemed like a long distance off, about the Rideau Canal Waterway.

I sat up, squinting and blinking, trying to clear my head.

"That's my bed you're on, technically."

I jumped a bit and kind of yelled. Not scared, just startled.

"*What* is *wrong* with you?" I demanded.

Lynn just laughed. She was curled up on the armchair across from me, brushing her hair.

"Well, it *is*," she said. "My bed, I mean."

"*Technically*," I said through gritted teeth, "this is *not* your bed. *This* is a couch, which you happen to be sleeping on these days because you're a loser with nowhere else to go."

"There are *plenty* of places I could go," she snapped.

"Name one."

"I could stay with friends — I have *lots* of friends you know — or go back to Conor, or rent my own apartment. To name a few."

I was about to shoot her answers apart when I remembered that I'd wanted to talk to her. So, I swallowed my annoyance and said, "Yeah, you're right. Sorry."

She looked suspicious for a few seconds, but then she relaxed and settled back in the chair again.

After a minute I mentioned that I could stand something to eat. She said she was kind of hungry, too, and we headed into the kitchen like a couple of combatants who'd formed a truce for the common good.

Lynn whipped up a couple of cheese omelettes; I made toast and we sat down to eat. I figured this was as good a time as any to find out what she knew.

chapter sixteen

"Do you remember anything about our father?"

Lynn's head jerked up at my question, panic written on her face.

"Are you crazy? We are *never* to talk about him," she whispered. Her eyes darted around as though there were hidden listeners.

"Why not?"

"Have you lost it altogether?" She looked around again. "Where's Mom?"

"I dunno. Out somewhere, I guess."

"Are you sure? I mean, how do you know she's not in her room lying down or something?" She leaned forward, looking past me. "Her door's shut ... she could be in there."

"Her shoes aren't here," I said, pointing to the doormat where she always slipped them off when she came in. "Just calm down."

"You haven't been through what I've been through," Lynn said, "so don't tell me to calm down. She goes ballistic if you even *mention* him."

"Was he *that* bad?"

"He was a monster! Why do you think Mom freaks out if you bring him up?"

"So you've tried to talk to her about him?"

"Not for years. It was too painful for Mom. She'd get more and more worked up until she was nearly beside herself and I didn't find anything out, anyway."

"But you must *remember* things about him. You were seven when they got divorced."

"It's kind of jumbled in my head."

"What do you mean?"

"I used to think I remembered a lot of things, but as I got older some of it got confused. Now, I can hardly tell which things I actually remember. A lot of it seems to be stuff Mom told me about."

"Like what?"

"Well, it's hard to sort things out sometimes. When I try to bring back the actual *details,* it's all messed up in my head. Mostly, I remember Mom telling me to be careful and how if I ever saw him I should scream and run. It bothers me that I can't remember clearly, but that's probably trauma from the things he did, you know?

I knew what she meant. It was exactly what had been bothering me lately.

"One time that I had to talk to a guy — I think he was a social worker, Mom went over and over the things Dad had done to me, so I'd remember what I had to tell him. Only, she said when I told about it I had to say *I* remembered it. Otherwise, the guy wasn't going to be able to protect me. But later, I heard her telling the social worker that *she* hadn't known this stuff was happening until after Dad moved out and *we* started telling *her* what had been going on. It sounded like she'd never seen it herself, but it felt like she had told *me* about it. Her voice seems to be in the background in a lot of my memories."

All of a sudden I felt as if someone had sunk a fist in my gut. "Mine are like that, too!" I told her. "It's as if they have her voice narrating them. I wish they were clearer."

"Yeah, well, you were pretty young," Lynn said. "And it must have been hard on Mom, having to talk about those things. She suffered so much. We all did. But, remember how she tried to make it better for us?"

"How?" I asked.

"Buying us things, taking us for ice cream or dough-nuts. Stuff like that."

"All parents do that," I said.

"Yes, but she always got us something special any-time we'd had to talk about *him*, and the things he did to us. She loved us so much. Not like *him*."

She looked like she was going to say more but she just swallowed hard a couple of times. Then she started crying.

I felt sick. What was I doing, anyway, getting her all worked up and bawling over stuff from the past? And why? Because my memories were hazy? Because there was someone watching me and I had a vague idea he *might* be my father?

"Hey," I said. I touched her arm. "Let's just forget it. I'm sorry I brought it up."

"No!" She whirled around and glared at me. "I do not want to forget it. I want to know—"

"What?"

"I'm not even sure. I've just always felt like there was more." A tear burst out of her right eye and skated off her cheek, exploding on the table. "Like there's some-thing missing and that if I just figure it out I can deal with it and stop having strange dreams and thoughts. I want the questions in my head to stop!"

"Me too, I guess," I admitted.

"I always told people I hated him," she said. Her eyes shifted to look down, away from me. "I said I never wanted to see him again."

"Yeah, so did I."

"But, sometimes ... I wonder about him."

"What?"

"I wonder ... if he ever thinks about me. I mean, us. Or why, in all the years since they broke up, he never got in touch, not even once."

"Maybe he didn't know where we were," I said, thinking again of the man who'd been watching me.

"I dream things that don't make sense sometimes," Lynn said. A hint of a smile struggled through for just a second. "I dream that I'm little and we're at the zoo and he's carrying me on his shoulders so I can see the animals better. And I feel so safe way up there."

Something leapt in my gut and a flash of a scene went by, a quick vision of being up in the air, running alongside a giraffe.

"Do you see any giraffes in your dream?" I asked.

"Giraffes? No, but *you* used to want to race them," she laughed. "You'd say, 'fasser, fasser' while Daddy ..."

Daddy.

Lynn's voice trailed off, her smile chased away by a look of panic. "I must have dreamed that, too," she said. She shook her head, like that would clear things up.

"I don't think so. It, I dunno, *felt* real, and I had a flash of something about it before you said that."

She let that sink in, which was fine with me. I had

my own thoughts — and questions — to contend with right then.

"Do you remember what he *looks* like?" I asked, breaking the silence at last.

"Kind of. I mean, I think I'd know him if I saw him." She took a deep breath and glanced nervously at the door, like Mom might be crouched listening on the other side of it.

"The wedding pictures are in Mom's room," she whispered.

"*What?*"

"The pictures from when they got married," she said. "Mom has them in an album in that filing cabinet in her room. Or, she used to, anyway."

"How do you know?"

"I saw them once when I was waiting for her to get my birth certificate. That was when I was applying for my social insurance number. I was sitting on her bed and she unlocked the cabinet and started digging through.

"I don't think she realized she'd put the album on the bed. She'd tossed a bunch of things there while she rifled through some papers in the bottom, and I picked up the album and opened it."

"Did she see you?"

"Yeah. After a minute or two she noticed and she just *freaked*. Grabbed it and screamed that I had no business touching her personal stuff. Her whole face turned red."

"I wonder where she keeps the key," I mused aloud. If I could get a look at that album, I might be able to tell if the guy following me was my dad.

"Yeah? Forget *that*. I've looked high and low for it."

"So you could see the pictures again?"

"Yeah." Lynn looked away, like she was embarrassed.

"It's too late to do anything tonight," I said. "She could walk in any time. But tomorrow, when she goes out, let's take another look."

"Sure," Lynn said, "but you won't find anything."

I didn't bother answering her, but I had a lot more confidence in myself than Lynn apparently had in me. I'd hidden a lot of things (okay, it was mostly weed) back when I had stuff to hide. I knew a lot more about hiding places than she did.

If the key to that cabinet was in Mom's room, I was going to find it.

chapter seventeen

"We'll be killed if we get caught."

We'd barely stepped through the doorway into Mom's room when Lynn offered this dire prediction. She was exaggerating but it *was* safe to say if Mom ever found us snooping around in her room there would be a scene bad enough and loud enough that the neighbours would be giving us strange looks for weeks.

"Don't worry so much," I said. I gave a wave of indifference to show her my total lack of concern.

"Boo!" she yelled, then laughed when I jumped.

"That was just reflexes," I said. "Now quit messing around and let's do this."

We got busy, searching carefully through all of the obvious places first. Even though we got fairly absorbed in our search, we flinched at every strange noise. For some reason there were a lot of them — sounds of footsteps in the hallway outside, keys turning in doors, creaking, rustling, and on and on. It was like the apartment had suddenly become haunted.

"You know," Lynn said after a particularly unnerving noise, "if she *does* come through that door, we don't have a prayer of getting out of here before she sees us."

It was true that the layout was working against us. The door to the apartment opened into the kitchen, with the living room just past it in one open space. The hallway to the bedrooms branched off from the kitchen, on your right just inside the door, and Mom's room was straight ahead at the end.

We'd talked about whether or not we should leave the door open or closed while we were in there. Open, Mom would definitely see it right away, because she always left it shut. Closed, we'd have even less time to cover our tracks if we didn't hear her until she opened the bedroom door and saw us there. Besides, being in there with the door closed would make us look even guiltier.

It took more than an hour to go through her dresser, carefully checking under and among the clothes, and pulling each drawer out to see if anything was secured to the bottom. We lifted the mattress on the bed, crawled underneath it and shone a flashlight at the underside of the box spring.

"She's going to know we were in here," Lynn said at one point. "There's no way she's not."

"Not if we're really careful about putting things back exactly as they were," I said, but I had an uneasy feeling she was right. I think I'd know it if someone went through my stuff, no matter how careful they tried to be.

"The key probably isn't even in here, anyway. I bet she keeps it in her purse or something."

"She might," I said, "but I think it's more likely to be here."

By then we'd finished with most of her stuff, looked in the light fixture, under the carpet edges, behind the baseboard heater, checked for loose trim around the doors and window, and lifted down the few pictures Mom had hanging to see if there was anything behind them.

Nothing.

"There's still the closet," I said after we'd searched the rest of the room. Neither of us was keen to start in there because it was crammed full of bags and boxes.

"We might as well get started." Lynn sighed. "It's going to take hours to go through this stuff."

But it didn't, because when we started to look, the first thing I noticed was that an old winter jacket Mom hadn't worn for years seemed out of place. Other things that were rarely worn — or retired — were all shoved to the back, but not this coat.

I reached in and felt around in the pockets. Nothing. Then I thought to check if there were any inside pockets. Sure enough there was one on the left side of the coat, and a small key was tucked into it.

I pulled it out and held it up for Lynn to see. She squealed and clapped her hands like a little kid and asked me how I'd known where to look.

I told her how I'd figured it out while we went to the filing cabinet and knelt in front. The key fit, and it was that simple — a twist and the cabinet was unlocked, along with all the secrets it held.

"You're going to think I'm nuts," I said to Lynn, but before we start looking at any of this, I think we should get a copy made of the key."

"You're joking, right?"

"No, I mean it. There might be stuff in here that we don't have time to look at today — stuff that's important. If she suspects we've been in her things — like you think she will — she might start to carry the key with her, or hide it somewhere we'd never look. The only way to make sure we're going to get a look at everything in here is if we have our own key."

"Okay," she said reluctantly. "But you go."

I agreed, relocked the cabinet against Lynn's protests (though it didn't take long to convince her that we'd be dead meat if Mom came along and it was unlocked) and took off for the hardware store three blocks away.

All the way there and back I kept telling myself that chances were good Mom wouldn't even come home while I was gone, much less happen to look for the key. Still, it was a relief when I got back to the apartment and Lynn reported that everything was okay.

We checked to make sure the copy worked, then put Mom's key back in her jacket pocket and closed the closet door.

My chest thumped heavily as we pulled open the cabinet's top drawer for the second time. It was stuffed full, cards we'd given Mom, old artwork and things like that, all jammed in — some of it organized and secured with rubber bands, some of it just in there loose.

We closed that without looking at any of it and slid the bottom drawer open. The album sat right on top, two lacy bells crossed over each other on the front. It had been white once, but was yellowed with age and handling.

I sucked in air and flipped it open.

There he was, standing next to Mom, smiling out at me from an eight by ten glossy.

My father.

I stood there looking and looking, like I might be able to see more than the surface image, until I became aware that Lynn was trembling beside me.

"That's him," she said, pointing at him like I needed that explained. "That's Daddy."

Daddy.

She tried to smile, still crying, and put her hand on my arm. Then she kind of sank against me and sobbed.

I put my arm around her (I'm not a total jerk) and held onto her until she got herself calmed down.

"It's okay," I said. My throat hurt.

It was a few minutes before Lynn pulled herself together enough to keep looking through the rest of the pictures. We stood there, flipping pages, because we didn't want to sit on the bed and we didn't dare leave the room. We might not be able to get out before Mom saw us, but at least we could try to shove the album back and lock the cabinet without her seeing what we were up to.

It was pretty strange, looking at this smiling person who had his arm around our mom. She was right up against his chest in a lot of the shots, looking, I dunno, *sheltered* somehow. I had a flash of déjà vu but it was gone before I could catch anything from it.

"Where do you think he is now?" Lynn asked when we'd finished turning all the pages and had gone back to the first one.

"Who knows," I said. I still wasn't ready to tell her about my suspicions.

Besides, I'd tried to compare his face to the guy who'd been following me, but too much time had passed for me to be certain. There was a resemblance, but I honestly couldn't say for sure if it was the same person.

I wondered, too, if I'd met him on the street and he'd looked exactly the same as he had when the pictures were taken, would I have known him? I had a feeling I would have. Even though I couldn't have brought up any kind of clear image in my head beforehand, as soon as I saw his picture I had an immediate and powerful sense of recognition.

After all, even though this guy was a stranger to me, he was still my father.

chapter eighteen

When we'd finished looking at the album, Lynn and I agreed we'd better not press our luck. We locked everything back up, closed the door to the room, and sat at the kitchen table for a while, just yakking.

But something happened to me while Lynn was talking. I don't think it was because of anything she said but I can't be sure because her words had stopped registering in my brain a few moments before.

It wasn't one of those times when I just drift off and don't listen. In fact, we'd been in the middle of a heavy discussion about whether it was possible to do self-hypnosis to make memories clearer. Mostly, we wondered if that would help us figure out if what we *thought* were memories could really be things we'd been told often enough that they *seemed* to be memories. For some reason, that question kept coming up over and over.

It was around that point in our discussion that I noticed Lynn's mouth was moving but something was wrong with her voice. Her words seemed to be coming out of a long tunnel — hollow-sounding with a bit of an echo. I realized I wasn't taking in anything she was saying and her voice sounded slow and garbled, like when something goes into slow motion on a movie.

Oblivious to this, she continued on. I watched her face, fascinated by the way her expression changed, going through an amazing range of emotions in what couldn't have been more than a couple of minutes — though it felt oddly timeless.

It made me think of parties I'd been to where someone would pass around brownies. Then, things would slow down and it would be like there was a thick glass barrier between me and everything around me. Sometimes I couldn't move at all for a while, and I'd get paranoid that there was going to be a fire and I wouldn't be able to move to get out.

I wondered, for just a few seconds, if I was having some kind of flashback, so I lifted my hand an inch or so to test that idea out. I thought I might not be able to move, but my hand worked okay.

Lynn was looking at me then, half scared and half puzzled. She'd finally realized something was wrong and had shut up long enough to check it out.

When she saw me focusing on her she started with the questions.

"What's wrong? Are you all right? Porter?"

"Stop," I said, surprised to find my voice working. "Don't talk right now."

"Do you feel sick? Maybe you need to lie down. Should I call someone?"

"Be quiet," I said. My voice was very, very calm. "I mean it."

"What is *wrong* with you? You're acting all weird and—"

"I said to *SHUT UP*," I roared. My fist came down on the table. The salt and pepper shakers jumped.

So did Lynn. I could see right away there were going to be more tears. Only, there was nothing in me right then that cared.

"I've gotta get out of here," I said, barely managing not to yell. I pushed my chair away from the table and turned so I didn't have to look at her stupid, crumpling face.

I grabbed my shoes and pulled them on. One of the laces broke when I yanked on it to tie them. I stuffed what was left of the lace under the tongue and left the apartment, slamming the door so hard I knew there'd be faces looking out from other apartments on our floor any second.

I wasn't in the mood to look at a bunch of morons who have nothing better to do than stick their heads into the hallway every time there's a noise, so I yanked open the door to the stairwell and descended the stairs in leaps and jumps, taking the half flights in two or three steps each.

Lester and Addie Phelps, an old couple that lived on the first floor, were just coming in when I reached the front door. They were nice people, the kind of old folks who were always fussing over each other.

Addie used to make mittens for the kids in the building, until her arthritis got too bad. And every summer on the last weekend in August they'd invite us all for hotdogs and Kool-Aid (which Lester called Freshie) and give us each a pencil for school.

Lester always made a little speech then, about education and how important it was and how he was held back in life because he never got the proper schooling.

"Now, each and every one of you is 'specially good at something," he'd say, when he was wrapping it up, "and Addie and me are darned proud of you — pardon my French. So we hope you'll have a real good year at school and learn your best and mind your teachers."

I used to hate it when Lester's speech was over.

Then we'd file out while Addie patted each of us on the head, like she was blessing us or something.

I still got invited, but I hadn't gone to their "Hot-dog 'N Freshie" parties for quite a few years. One of them always tracked me down later, though, and told me they were sorry I hadn't been able to make it, and gave me a pencil.

When I was a lot younger, I used to think it would be cool to have grandparents like the Phelpses. I'd imagine having someone like Lester giving me speeches regular — not just once a year with a group, but stuff he'd say just for me. Or Addie, making me cookies and reading me stories and whatever other things grandparents do.

My mom's father died when I was nine and her mom had been in a nursing home as long as I'd known her, so she didn't really count. She cried all the time and smelled funny. I hated to let her touch me when I was little, because she'd get hold of my shirt and wouldn't let go. Mom only went once a year herself and she had stopped making me go with her when I was around twelve.

As for my dad's family, I didn't know anything about them, not even if they were living, or where, or any of that stuff.

Anyway, getting back to this particular day — the Phelpses were coming in and, since they didn't exactly move fast, I had to stand back and wait for them. I forced what I hoped was a friendly expression onto my face, though I could still feel my jaws clamped together.

"Porter, dear, how are you?" Addie asked, pausing right in the doorway.

"Good, thanks. You?" I managed a tight smile.

"Well, now, I can't complain. At this age if a body can still get around, that's about the best you can hope for."

"You're not *that* old," Lester said to her. "Still young enough to be my girl, anyway."

"Oh, you old flatterer," she said. Her hand went out in his general direction and swatted the air, missing him entirely.

"Yeah, well, that's good," I said. I wished I could grab them and haul them into the building so I could get by. "But, I kind of have to go somewhere." My face hurt from the effort of holding a smile.

"Oh, my dear!" Addie said. "Did you hear that, Lester? We're holding Porter up. He probably has a girl waiting for him and here we are on about nothing like two doddering old fools."

"No, no, it's just that I *do* have to go."

They shuffled in, spilling out apologies and reminding me about the party the next month and saying how they really hoped I'd be able to make it that year.

"Yeah, thanks. I'll try," I lied. At last they were in and I could escape.

I hit the sidewalk jogging, feeling a bit guilty for offing Lester and Addie that way. They faded from my thoughts within minutes, though, and I found myself running faster and faster, hands clenched into fists, gulping air and fighting whatever it was that was rising up in my chest.

It wasn't panic, though the way I was running it almost seemed like it might be. A few minutes passed before I realized it was anger. The kind of anger that's so powerful it could burn a hole right through you.

The strange thing was, I had no idea who or what I was angry at.

I ran, shoving myself forward, stunned by the strength of my growing rage. It felt like something living — a separate force pulsing and writhing in my body but not exactly part of me.

My throat and eyes burned and my teeth hurt from being clenched. I kept running. I passed The Singing Cane, was vaguely aware of Rodney sticking his head out the door and calling my name. I didn't turn or even pause.

My feet moved faster and faster and I felt as though I could keep going until I got out of the city, until I found an open field somewhere. I pictured myself in the middle of nowhere, lifting my head up and howling like a wolf.

It was getting hard to breathe but I kept going long past the point when my chest started to ache — past when it felt like it would explode.

I didn't stop until it got so that I couldn't suck in enough air to fuel my body with the oxygen it needed.

When I did finally slow down and quit, my legs became instant rubber and refused to hold me. I leaned, gasping for air, against a building — an old stone place with streaks of black and cracks in the foundation.

I'd zigzagged a good deal in order to avoid stopping for cars or traffic lights, so I wasn't sure exactly where I was. Not that it mattered. I couldn't have cared less.

After a few minutes the anger had receded a good deal, leaving me a bit more clear-headed than I'd been earlier. But I just stayed there, sagging against the wall, trying to figure out what had happened.

I couldn't remember ever being that upset before, not even in the middle of a fight. Not even the time I'd been down and two guys were kicking me, and it had made me furious enough to get me back onto my feet and into the fight.

The only thing I could figure was that there must be some stuff buried in my subconscious — stuff I couldn't remember but that had been triggered by seeing my father's picture.

I thought about those pictures, and wished I knew for sure if he and the Watcher were the same person. It strengthened my resolve to corner him somehow and get some answers to what was going on.

If, in fact, he *was* my father, I had some other questions for him, too.

chapter nineteen

It was a while before I was ready to head home, and when I did, I took my time, ambling along the street and trying to ignore the fact that I was getting really hungry. That was no easy task since I passed a hotdog vendor, a sub place, two Italian restaurants, and a Tim Hortons before I'd even made it halfway.

Thoughts of food were driven right out of my head when I happened to glance to the right and see Lavender Dean coming out of a ladies' clothing store. She saw me, waved, and smiled.

"Hey, Porter."

"Hi."

"You going somewhere?"

"Not really. Just hangin'."

She looked *good*, and I thought about how she'd been so sweet and friendly the last time I'd seen her at

Pockets. Something about Lavender filled up my head — the shape of her mouth and the way her nose squeezed into a crinkle when she giggled. Stuff like that can get in your brain and make you do stupid things if you're not careful.

"I'm just heading to my place," she said. "You want to come and hang out for a while?"

"Uh, sure. I'm not doing anything, anyway." I could almost hear Tack laughing and telling me how *smooth* I was.

Her building was just a short distance away and we walked there without talking at all. To tell the truth, I was so happy to be walking beside her that I didn't feel the need for conversation. Anyway, that would have been a distraction from the side view I had of her movements — the slight sway in her walk, how she moved all smooth and liquid.

A couple of times she turned slightly and smiled at me. I think she meant to put me at ease, but all it did was make my stomach lurch nervously. It was a relief when we got to her place and flopped on the couch — one of those big sectional kinds, so soft that you sink right in when you sit down.

"I'm starving," she said, kicking her shoes off and letting them drop to the floor. "I think I'll make a sandwich. Want one?"

"Yeah. Sure. Thanks."

She dug through the fridge and came out with enough stuff for a dozen sandwiches, piling cold sliced meats and cheeses along with bread, lettuce, tomato, cucumber, onion, and pickles on the table.

"Come and help yourself," she said, putting plates out. I joined her in the kitchen and grabbed a couple of slices of bread out of the bag while she sliced the tomato.

"By the way, I saw you earlier," she said as we slapped stuff onto slices of bread. "You want mustard? Mayo?"

"Mayo, thanks." I tried to read her face while she passed me the jar. "Did you say you saw me *today*?"

"Yeah. You looked like the hounds of hell were after you." She took a huge bite of her sandwich and made *Mmm* sounds while she chewed.

"Oh, that." I laughed but it came out sounding more like a croak. "I was, uh, jogging."

"I don't *think* so," she said. "You looked pretty upset."

"Where were you? When you saw me?"

"At work. That store I was in when you came along — I work there part-time."

"Oh, yeah? Cool. How long you been working there?"

"A few months. And are you trying to change the subject?" Without waiting for an answer, she added, "I thought you looked like you could use someone to talk to."

146

"Nothing to talk about," I said. An uncomfortable thought occurred to me. "Is that why you asked if I wanted to come here?"

"No. Yeah. I dunno, maybe."

"Well, sorry to disappoint you, but I was just running."

"Really?"

"Yeah, really."

She narrowed her eyes and studied me while she took a few more bites, chewed and swallowed.

"Nope," she said after a minute. "You're lying."

I didn't know how to answer that. She *was* right but I wasn't in the mood to tell her so.

"I guess it's none of my business, anyway," she said.

That could have saved me from having to think too hard about what to say, except I noticed her chin rose a little and I could see she was going to get sulky — go around with a long face for who knows how long.

Seemed like it might be better to just go ahead and tell her something.

"I think my father is following me," I said. Right away I realized that probably wasn't the best opening line I could have come out with, but it chased off her pout.

"You were running because your *father* was chasing you?" she asked, her eyes all round and cute.

"No, no, I was just, uh, jogging to, uh, clear my head," I said. "You know, think about some stuff."

147

"So your father *wasn't* following you?"

"Yeah. Well, I mean, I think he has been, but not right then. I'm not even sure about it, anyway, but some guy has been, and I think it might be him."

"What, was he in disguise or something?" she asked. She looked confused, but also kind of sympathetic and, sort of soft. And she leaned toward me and put her hand on my arm.

So, that's how, without meaning to, I ended up telling Lavender the whole story. She listened while I told her about The Watcher and how Lynn and I had broken into my mom's cabinet to find the pictures.

"You mean you didn't even know what your own father looked like?" she asked. Her hand squeezed my arm a little.

"Nope. Not before today."

"That must bite," she said. "What did he do that was so terrible?"

"He yelled at me and my sister, and slapped us and stuff."

"Yelled, and slapped you?" she echoed.

"Yeah, when we were little."

"And that's why you haven't seen him *since*?"

"Not once."

"That doesn't sound right," she said. She shook her head. "I mean, it doesn't seem like enough of a reason for you to have never seen him since you were a little kid."

"Yeah, well, we didn't *want* to see him. My mom says we used to scream if anyone even mentioned his name."

"That sounds kind of like..." Her voice trailed off and she dropped her hand to her side.

"Like what?"

"It's not really my place to say, but it just sounds so much like the same thing that's happening with my cousin, Kenny."

"Which is what?"

"He and his wife — I should say ex-wife now — had a little boy four years ago, and when he was about two they split up. Now she's telling everyone that Simon, their kid, is terrified of his father, and Kenny is having a terrible time getting to see his son.

"The worst thing is that Simon says Kenny did things to him – terrible things – like he pushed him down the stairs, only there's *no way* any of it is true. You should have seen him with that kid — he was crazy about him. And Kenny wouldn't hurt a fly, much less his own son."

"Why would the kid make stuff like that up?" I asked.

"There's only one *possible* answer," Lavender told me. "Simon's mother brainwashed him, to hurt Kenny and keep them apart. She programmed that poor kid to believe his father did awful things to him, so now Simon is scared of his own father."

I stared at her.

"That didn't happen with me and Lynn," I said coldly. "Do you think my mom's crazy or something? She wouldn't do something like that."

"Okay, sorry. I didn't mean to accuse your mother of anything. It just sounded a lot like —"

"It's *nothing* like that," I said.

"So, forget I even mentioned it." She smiled tentatively and touched my arm again.

"Don't worry about it," I said. I shoved my anger aside and reminded myself that she was just trying to be helpful.

"Hey, I know what will loosen you up," she said, taking my hand and tugging me with her through the living room. Sliding glass doors opened onto a small concrete balcony and she pulled me out onto it.

Then she reached into her jeans and the next thing she was holding a spliff. She lit it, took a pull, and held it out to me.

chapter twenty

I don't remember my mouth ever going as dry as it did while I stood looking at the joint Lavender was holding out toward me. The smell rising from it told me it was pure bud.

It was by no means the first time I'd been offered weed since I quit toking, but it was one of the hardest. I shook my head and told myself I wasn't tempted.

"You sure? It's killer stuff."

"Yeah, I can see that."

"One hit?" she sucked in another lungful and held it, waiting for my answer.

"Look, I used to have a problem with this," I said. "I don't care what anyone else does, but I leave it alone now."

Lavender shrugged and leaned back against the balcony railing, closing her eyes. She exhaled, a quick burst of smoke that broke up fast, took a third toke and squeezed the lit end to extinguish it. She pulled a folded piece of foil from her pocket, wrapped it and stuck it all back in her pocket.

I saw her body relaxing; a dreamy smile drifted across her face. Her eyes sparkled and shone.

"C'mere," she said, holding a hand toward me.

I closed the short gap between us, felt her arms slide up around my neck, and leaned down to kiss her.

After a couple of minutes, I backed into the apartment, still holding her against me. We moved over to the couch but all of a sudden she pulled away and sprawled back.

"Give me a foot massage?" she said. She stuck one up and wiggled her toes.

"Uh, okay." I'd never given a foot massage and I've gotta say the request was coming at a pretty strange time, but I was game. "What do I do?"

She gave me a few instructions at first but then stopped talking and murmured happy *Mmm* sounds while I rubbed her feet. I figured I was doing an okay job of it by the little noises she was making.

I was starting to worry that maybe this was going to put her to sleep, since she was getting more and more drowsy and relaxed looking. I tried talking to her but she didn't answer and I was casting about in my head for some other way of waking her up without getting her mad, when the apartment door opened.

A pair of teens came into the kitchen. I recognized the guy as Lavender's brother Mick. He's a year ahead of us in school. The girl on his arm looked to be a few years younger, though she'd done her best to pass as older than she was. She had on a short, tight black skirt, a thin yellow shirt that left a roll of belly exposed, and some kind of shoes with big platforms. She seemed to be wearing an awful lot of makeup, though I don't actually know much about that stuff. I do know that there was a lot of gunk on her eyes, and her mouth was almost the colour of her skirt, which you'd hope wasn't the way the poor kid was born. She walked with a slinky sort of sway that might have been sexy if it had been even slightly natural.

"Hey Mick, hey Arlene," Lavender said. At least their entrance had drawn her back to the land of the living.

"Yeah, hi. Do you know where Mom and Dad are?" Mick said.

"Dunno, I just got home half an hour ago myself. Oh, uh, this is Porter. Mick, Arlene."

We all mumbled greetings and then Mick said he'd been hoping one of his parents would be home because he needed some cash. And — like a sudden afterthought — did *Lavender* have any money? She answered that she was broke.

Mick shot a couple of glances my way and for a second I thought he was going to ask *me* for money.

Twice he started to speak but I guess some remaining speck of dignity fought against it because his voice trailed off after he'd gotten out half a word.

"You got any smoke?" Arlene asked. I saw that she had the attitude younger kids put out there when they're trying to sound tough and sophisticated. It never works. In her case, she came across as hostile — for no reason.

"Nope," Lavender lied.

"That gram is gone *already?*" Mick asked. He frowned at me like I must have smoked it.

"Back off, Mick," Lavender said lazily.

He glared at her and then grumbled that he was going to get some CDs to listen to at some guy named Allen's place.

After he disappeared down the hall, Arlene let out a sigh and then came into the living room and plunked down on the arm of the couch. She had her lips stuck out in what my ex-girlfriend used to call the "Angelina Jolie pose." It made her look like a pouting two-year-old.

"I could *really* use a little something to get me right," she said. "We were at a party last night — it was totally sick — and anyway, this guy there had some blow that was barely stepped on. We got completely wrecked. It was insane but I'm feeling a bit sketchy today."

I'd been wondering why neither Mick nor Arlene had noticed that Lavender was high, but that pretty much explained it. They were too fogged to think about anything except getting smoothed out.

Lavender murmured a couple of sympathetic things after Arlene had unburdened her sad story, but she also made a point of catching my eye, winking, and casually tapping the pocket that held the remains of her spliff.

Mick seemed to take his time picking out the CDs and Arlene took that opportunity to roll her eyes upward and yawn. I assume she meant to let us know how bored she was to be sitting there instead of doing the cool doper things she usually did.

"Let's go," Mick said, when he finally reappeared. He jerked his head toward the door and Arlene shoved herself to her feet and walked heavily in that direction.

They'd barely shut the door behind them when Lavender turned to me. "Alone at last," she said, then added a low, throaty, "mu-wah-ha-ha!"

"Yes, at last," I said. I laughed in a way that was supposed to sound lecherous in a joking way. Instead, it came out like someone a bit demented.

Lavender giggled and shifted to a sitting position. I was all for that, but before I could even get my arm around her she was on her feet.

"We need music!" she said. "To dance."

"Uh …" I hesitated, not really wanting to refuse, but knowing there was no way I was going to get up and dance. I really suck at it.

"You wanna join … or *watch*?" she asked. Her eyes were wet and shining. "'Cause I wouldn't mind showing you this dance I invented."

"Go," I said, glad to have a way out handed to me.

"I call this 'Roastin' the Ghetto Bootie,'" she said, making it sound like a big announcement.

"*Roastin' the Ghetto Bootie*? Serious?"

"Uh-huh. Watch," she said as she made a music selection.

"Travelin' Band" — an old CCR tune — came blasting out a few seconds later and Lavender turned, put a finger to her lips and then proceeded with, as she called it, Roastin' the Ghetto Bootie.

It was like she half exploded, twitching and spazzing all over the place. It seemed that there were more arms and legs flying around than one girl could possibly have and I had to duck a few times or I'd have been clobbered.

When it was over she clapped for herself, jumping up and down like a little kid. I smiled watching her, clapped, too, and whistled, and wished she'd come over and sit with me again.

She did — so, naturally her mother chose that moment to come through the door. Lavender introduced us and Mrs. Dean told me it was nice to meet me and that she wished she'd known Lavender was going to have a friend over because she'd have planned dinner to include me, instead of bringing home just enough take-out for the family.

The invitation to leave didn't bother me a bit. I headed home feeling good about how things had gone with Lavender. That lasted about half a block. Then I started thinking about some of the things I'd managed to push off to the side while I'd been with her.

By the time I got to my place, the questions had flooded back in.

Was the Watcher my father? And what did he want?

chapter twenty-one

Lynn was acting weird when I got home. Or, I should say, she was acting absolutely normal, which in itself was weird, because she didn't mention a single word about the way I'd freaked and stormed out earlier. And trust me, Lynn is *not* the type to let something like that go.

Normally, she'd have dug for it until I either fed her a lie to shut her up, or got *really* mad, or (as happens in rare situations) actually told her what she wanted to know. Just to get her off my back.

But that time, nothing. I knew it could only mean she was up to something herself, and I was right. I hadn't been home for fifteen minutes when she came over to where I was sitting on the couch, and cleared her throat. With Lynn, throat clearing is a sure sign that she's about to ask me for a favour. I pretended I didn't hear her.

Mom, who was home for a change, tried to give me a signal. I acted oblivious to that, too.

"Uh, Porter?" Lynn said when she saw I wasn't going to bite.

"Yeah?"

"I just wanted to mention that, uh, Conor is coming over."

"*Conor?*"

"Yeah. I invited him for dinner. And I'd like a nice, pleasant meal without anyone bringing up things that might cause trouble."

"Such as?" Like I didn't know.

"You know, like Daryl. You won't mention that I was out with him, will you?"

I was tempted to tell her, yeah, I *would* mention it. If she wanted to go around acting like some kind of skank, she should expect him to find out about it.

But then I got a flash of her that morning, bawling her head off with her whole body shaking and shuddering.

"Yeah, okay. Don't worry about it," I said.

"Thanks!" She hugged me and looked relieved. "'Cause he should be here any minute."

It was actually another twenty minutes before he showed up and by then Lynn had started to pace and run back and forth to the living room window to see if she could spot him coming along the sidewalk. I could tell she was getting worried that he wasn't coming.

I'd started to worry a bit myself. After all, if they patched things up she'd be moving back out. It hadn't been the worst thing in the world having her around, but I wouldn't be sorry to see her leave, either. Get things back to normal.

When Conor finally got there he had a bouquet of flowers for her. Lynn went on a bit more than necessary, considering it was just one of those cheap mixed bouquets from a grocery store. I heard her whisper, "You really *do* love me," to him and that made me feel like speaking up and telling her she shouldn't need flowers to tell her that — she should know it from the fact that the guy had been putting up with her for years. But they were hugging and looking sappy so I kept it to myself.

We all sat down at the table then and Lynn started dishing up the food. I could see she'd done her best to make a fancy meal. Unfortunately, the cheese sauce was thick and lumpy and the vegetables she poured it over were limp and soggy. Besides that, she'd made scalloped potatoes which, judging by the burnt smell in the apartment, had boiled over in the oven. The last item on the table was ham — one of those round things sliced down the middle. She'd stuck pineapple slices all around the outside of it and at least it looked okay.

Conor told Lynn that the food smelled great, which it might have if we'd actually been able to smell it over the burned milk in the oven. He dragged me into the lie by adding, "doesn't it, Porter?"

"Yeah, great," I said. Lynn started to stick her tongue out at me but rearranged it into a smile when Conor happened to glance over at her.

There was a lot of smiling going on, in fact, and a little hand-holding under the table. Lynn looked happy and I was glad for her. I just wished she hadn't gone out with that other guy. It made me feel like I was lying to Conor.

While we ate, Mom kept commenting about how nice it was to see Conor and what a good guy he was and how she'd always said so. Just a shade different from the tune she'd been singing when Lynn came home, as I recalled.

I wondered, a couple of times, how Conor could be sitting there swallowing all of this without realizing that something was a shade off. But it wasn't my problem and when I thought about it later, it occurred to me that maybe he *did* know, on some level, that things weren't quite genuine. And maybe he decided to just let whatever it was go, and play along with the act.

After we'd eaten, I called Tack's place, but his kid brother Lemon (his name is actually Lemuel but everyone calls him Lemon) told me he had gone somewhere with Teisha.

Suddenly restless, I couldn't see hanging around the apartment, so I decided to kick around the neighbourhood for a while, maybe drop by Pockets later on. I'd just started down the hall when Lynn called me back.

"Phone for you," she said. "Some girl."

"Hello?" I said, hoping it was Lavender. It was.

"You doing anything?" she asked.

"Not really. I was just going to take a walk, see if anyone was around."

"Why don't you come by my place and I'll go with you."

"Sure." I hung the phone up and turned to see Lynn watching me with a dumb smile, like she knew a big secret. She caught me before I could get back out the door.

"Someone special?" she asked very softly. I knew she was keeping it down so Mom wouldn't start with the questions. She always gives me the third degree when I'm seeing someone.

"Just a girl," I said. "She's okay."

"Well, anyway, have a good time." Then she hugged me, real quick.

It took me fifteen minutes or so to get to Lavender's place. I found her out in front of the building sitting on a bench waiting. She jumped up to meet me on the walk and something in her movement reminded me of the funny dance she'd done that afternoon.

"Hey," I said when she got close. I could smell her shampoo.

"You rescued me," she said, falling into step beside me. "My mom's gone to her sister's place for the evening and my dad rented an old movie. He was trying to persuade me to watch it with him."

"Do you two watch movies together very often?"

"Yeah, sure. But it depends on the show. He talked me into watching *Apocalypse Now* one time and I swear it was the most depressing thing I've ever seen."

"The *horror*!" I said, in what seemed to me a passable imitation of Brando in that film. It had been the only thing on TV one night, so I'd watched it. I thought it was pretty good.

Apparently, that particular part hadn't made much of an impression on Lavender. She looked at me nervously.

"From the movie," I explained. "*Apocalypse Now*."

"Oh, right." She smiled but I could see she had something else on her mind. It didn't take long for her to bring it up.

"You religious or something?"

"Religious?" The question startled me. It was the last thing I'd expected from her. "Not really. I mean, I believe in God, I guess, but we don't go to church or anything."

"I was just wondering, uh, about this afternoon."

"You mean because I didn't get high with you?"

"Yeah. I know what you told me, but I thought there might have been more to it than that."

"Nope. That was the whole thing. I had a bit of trouble with it a while back — I was messing up a lot. I had to quit."

"Oh." She fell silent for a minute. Then she said, "I don't toke that much."

I wasn't sure what kind of response she was looking for there.

"Like, when I told Mick I'd smoked the whole gram, that wasn't true. I just wasn't passing it over to them. I still have more than half of it left."

"Yeah? When did you get it?" If it was, like yesterday or something, that was nothing to brag about.

"I'm not sure. One day last week."

The joint she'd smoked earlier had been slender enough that for sure she'd be getting six of them out of a gram. If she smoked three of them in a week that could still mean she was getting high every day, assuming she just smoked half at a time, like she had in the afternoon.

"Why?" It was like she could hear me thinking it through. "Is that a problem?"

"It's not a problem for me," I said.

"I mean, I don't *have* to do it. I'm not a big stoner or anything."

I thought of how cute she'd been doing her silly Roastin' the Ghetto Bootie dance. Of how she'd beckoned me to her on the balcony and how her mouth had parted lazily when I kissed her. I wondered how much of that was her and how much was the weed.

"If you were thinking of hanging around, that is," she added, breaking into my thoughts.

"Yeah, I was — if you wanted me to," I said. "And it's no big deal either way. I'm not telling anyone what to do."

She smiled and stepped in a bit closer, touching the back of her hand against mine. I took hold of it, and right away she made her trademark little *Mmm* sound.

Everything was perfect. And then I saw him.

chapter twenty-two

I must have stiffened up because Lavender turned to me right away with questioning eyes and asked what was wrong.

"That's the guy who's been following me," I said, "the one coming out of Won Stop."

Won Stop is a combination convenience store and Chinese take-out. Nothing fancy — just basic things like egg rolls, fried rice, chow mien, and stuff like that, ready to serve from a hot buffet table.

The Watcher had emerged from there with a newspaper rolled up under one arm and a brown paper bag clutched in the opposite hand. He gave himself away almost immediately by looking over at me. When he saw that I was staring straight at him, he looked away in a quick, jerky movement.

"That's your father?" Lavender asked.

"I don't know. Not for sure. But he's been following me for a while."

"It *looks* like he's just getting something to eat," she said doubtfully.

"That's the kind of thing he does to, you know, cover up. But I catch him all the time. He's a bit of an amateur." Like I was used to being followed by professionals. "You keep watching and you'll see. He'll give himself away by looking at me."

The words were hardly out of my mouth when he took another quick glance my way, just like he'd done a minute before.

"So, let's go talk to him," she said.

"What?"

"Let's go talk to him. Tell him you know he's been watching you and find out what his game is. If that's your father, you want to know for sure, right?"

Something happened to my determination to talk to this guy. I *did* want to know, but my stomach clenched at the thought of talking to him. I suddenly realized that I wasn't as ready as I'd thought. Not yet.

"Hurry up," Lavender urged, pulling me along with her, "he's going to get away."

It was true he was walking quickly, heading toward my street. I figured he knew we'd made him, and he was planning the same dumb ruse he'd used before, pretending he lived in the building on my street.

"I'm pretty sure I know where he's headed," I said, even though I knew full well that if he went into the building it would be hard to find him again until he came back out. That was fine with me. It would buy me time without forcing me to admit my reservations to Lavender.

But with her propelling me along we kept gaining on him. By the time he turned off the sidewalk toward the building (just as I'd predicted), he was only about ten feet ahead of us.

There was nothing I could do as Lavender dragged me forward, through the lobby and over to the elevators.

I have to say the guy looked nervous when we got into the elevator with him. Lavender nudged me and I knew she meant I should say something, but my throat had constricted and I couldn't have spoken if I'd wanted to, which I didn't.

We stopped at the seventh floor and, with an uneasy glance in our direction, the guy stepped off. Right behind him was Lavender, who didn't notice I hadn't followed until it was too late. Frozen in place, I caught a glimpse of her startled face as the doors slid the last couple of inches and closed completely. And then it was moving — a slight lurch and it continued upward with me still on board.

I swear, I hadn't planned to do that — it just worked out that way. So there I was, rising alone through the building, totally numb. It could have been happening to someone else.

I couldn't believe how close I'd just come, or that, after spending so much time thinking about it, I'd (I might as well admit it) chickened out at the last second. The hard part was that — if that *was* my father — I had no idea what to expect. I'd never sat down in a room with him. We'd never had a conversation — not that I could remember, anyway.

All I knew was that he was a horrible person who'd mistreated me and Lynn. That was about the sum of it. Oh, yeah, and, as I'd heard many times, he'd never paid child support. Seems that for years every time I asked for *anything* that was the reason I couldn't have it.

Money didn't matter much at the moment, but the rest of it did. I was interested in knowing why he'd done the things he'd done, and then walked out and never even dropped a postcard in the mail, or picked up the phone to say hi.

But I had other questions, too. Like, had he taken me and Lynn to the zoo? Had we raced giraffes?

And, had we ever finger painted together? I don't know where that one came from, but it was in my head and I figured I might as well ask if I ever got the chance.

And what would I *call* him, if he was my father? Dad? Steve? Mr. Delancy? Nothing felt right but maybe something would if we were ever face-to-face.

The elevator stopped with a ping at the tenth floor and a woman got on. She glanced at me, summed me up, and looked straight ahead while still keeping track of me peripherally. I could feel it in the way she stood and stared forward without actually focusing on anything in front of her.

We started to descend. I looked at the number pads and willed myself to push the seven but my arm hung immobile at my side.

But seven lit up anyway and the elevator shuddered to a halt. I guessed Lavender had summoned it, and sure enough, when the door opened she was right there, eyes blazing. She reached in, grabbed me by the shirt, and unceremoniously hauled me out.

"*What* are you doing?" she demanded.

"I forgot to get off," I said. She looked at me like I'd lost my mind completely.

"Sorry," I added. I wasn't, though. All I felt was relief that the guy was nowhere in sight. Since Lavender had been forced to wait there for me, he'd had ample opportunity to take off. "Anyway, we can try another time."

"We're going *right now* and you're going to talk to him," she said. "I saw which apartment he went into."

"He went into an apartment?" Confusion swept over me. "But ..."

"Obviously, he lives here," she said, rolling her eyes. "Did it ever occur to you that he might have found out where you were and moved to be close to you?"

It hadn't.

"It makes sense," she added. "That way he could keep an eye out to see when you go by. Otherwise, he'd have to hang out in the streets all the time."

She was right. It did make sense.

"Now come *on*. You need to do this. Besides, I'm here." The last was said in a soft, almost shy voice, and she reached out and took my hand.

"I feel kinda sick," I said. "I might need to throw up."

"Suck it up, Princess," she snapped. "You are *not* getting out of this."

"You're mean," I said, but actually her cuteness was distracting me. She had this fierce look on her face like she might have fit right in with some ancient warrior tribe.

Not only that, but she was tricky, too. She'd been drawing me along without me even realizing it, and all of a sudden we'd stopped in front of a door.

"This is it," she said. "Now, knock!"

"Yeah, but, uh, I was thinking ... he's eating right now. Remember, the take-out from Won Stop?"

"I know you're probably scared, Porter," Lavender said gently. "And I don't blame you — anyone would be. But you've gotta find out, and waiting isn't going to make it easier."

I was searching my brain for something to say back (mainly, to deny the part about being scared) when the door we were standing in front of suddenly swung open.

The guy stood there, looking at me like he was waiting for something. Lavender poked me in the back with a sharp fingernail, which is not the nicest way to give someone a nudge.

"Can I help you?" the man asked after a minute had passed.

I found myself staring at him, comparing his face to the one in the album Lynn and I had looked at — could it have just been that morning? I couldn't seem to decide if it was the same person or not.

"Uh," I finally found my voice, "I was, uh, just wondering … are you my father?"

He didn't answer right away but after a few seconds' pause he stepped back a bit from the doorway.

"I think you'd better come in," he said.

chapter twenty-three

We followed him into the kitchen and sat down at a big wooden table. He asked if we wanted a glass of milk, or juice, or anything. I said I'd like some water.

As he put the glass down in front of me, he said, "First thing we need to clear up — my name is Nathan Sanning and I am most definitely *not* your father. Now, do you want to tell me who you are, and where this idea came from?"

I told him my name as his words sank in. I felt nothing. Not relief, not disappointment, not a thing. I think some part of me had probably already known.

"And I'm Lavender Dean. Porter's, uh, girlfriend," Lavender said.

Sanning was waiting for me to answer the rest of his question but I had one of my own instead.

"So, then, why have you been following me?"

"*I've* been following *you*?" If he wasn't genuinely surprised, he was quite an actor.

"Yeah. I've caught you at it a few times," I said, recounting some of the times I'd seen him lurking around, watching me.

"I'd gone in there to use the men's room," he explained, when I mentioned the day he'd been watching me from the restaurant. "It was hot out, so I was watching for the streetcar inside, where it was cool.

"I moved to this neighbourhood about three months ago," he continued. "And I *did* begin to take note of you — but that was because *you* kept looking at *me*. I assumed that you had mistaken me for someone you knew and would soon realize your mistake. Even so, it seemed that everywhere I turned, there you were, staring at me. It was a bit unsettling."

I felt like such a moron. Hearing Mr. Sanning explain it, I could see how I'd let my imagination invent a situation that had never existed.

"I'm sorry about this," I said. "It's just that you kind of look like my dad. I haven't seen him since I was four, but I must have remembered things about him without even knowing it. I guess some of it came out when I saw you."

"You have no contact with your father?"

"None. And that's the way I like it."

"But *can* you contact him — if you want to?"

"I *don't* want to."

"That's interesting because, based on what just happened, it appears that on some level — subconscious it seems — you're actually *looking* for your father."

"No way," I said. "I almost never even *thought* about him until all of this happened."

"That's my point. There was no reason for you to jump to the conclusion you did unless some part of you *wanted* to see him."

"Yeah, well, I don't think so. From what I've heard, he's not exactly Father of the Year."

"From what you've *heard*?"

"And what I remember. It's not all that clear. Like I said, I was only four the last time he was around."

"Do you have any older siblings?"

"A sister. She's nineteen. She was seven when our father split."

"What are her memories?"

"Same as mine, pretty much — that he was mean and didn't love us. My mom is the one who always took care of us."

"Do you and your sister remember *specific* things your father did that were mean?"

"Sure. He used to put us down and yell at us. He slapped Lynn on the head one time. And I remember him throwing me against a wall when I was one year old."

"When you were *one?*"

His tone told me he doubted I could remember something from that age, but I knew what I knew. I levelled a hard look at him but didn't answer.

Sanning cleared his throat. "Are there a lot of other memories like this?"

"A few. Why? What difference does it make?"

"Most children who have been abused by a parent still *want* to see them."

"That's stupid," I said, wondering what he was getting at.

"It's true, though. They long for a better relationship, for affection and closeness, in spite of the fact that hurtful things have been done to them."

"What's your point?" For some reason, I was starting to feel annoyed.

"It's just that it's possible there's more to your situation than you realize."

"What do you mean?"

He spoke slowly then, and I could see him choosing his words carefully. "The fact is that sometimes one parent will turn the children against the other parent after a breakup. In extreme cases, the children refuse to have anything to do with the parent they've been turned against."

"My mother didn't do that," I said angrily.

"I'm not accusing anyone of anything," Sanning claimed, "but one of the biggest red flags that this *may* have happened is when children want nothing to do with a parent they believe has abused them. Like I said, children who have actually been abused normally still want a relationship with the abuser. It's the children who have been deliberately turned against a parent who don't."

I stared at him in silence, my anger growing. He took this as a sign that he should keep talking.

"If it's even a possibility, I think it's important that you're aware of it. Look it up. It's called Parental Alienation."

"My mother took care of us. She did everything for me and my sister!" I said, fighting to stay calm. "It's my dirtbag of a father who hurt us and then took off and never looked back."

"It doesn't sound like you have any doubts," Sanning said. "I don't hear any sign of mixed feelings, that's for sure."

"Because I *have* none," I said, glad he was finally getting it.

"Lack of ambivalence is another strong sign of alienation."

"What?"

"Children who have been alienated generally don't have mixed feelings toward both parents — which is normal. Instead, they basically see one as all good and the other as all bad. I guess you're smart enough to figure out if that's true in your case."

"It's *not*."

"Okay. I'm sorry if I'm out of line here."

"You're *way* out of line," I said.

"Are you a psychiatrist or something?" Lavender asked.

"No, I'm a group home director. But I've seen a number of cases of Parental Alienation."

He turned back to me. "Look, Porter, I'm not saying that's what happened to you. I'm just saying it's *possible*. You owe it to yourself to find out the truth."

"This is *garbage*," I said, getting to my feet. Lavender kind of jumped, and I realized I'd yelled. I lowered my voice. "I'm outta here. Are you coming?"

She stood and followed me — out the door, down the hall, into the elevator, through the lobby, and outside — without a word. I could tell she was dying to say something and I knew it wasn't going to be something I wanted to hear.

"Look, Porter," she said finally, her voice hesitant but determined.

"I *really* don't want to talk about this anymore," I said.

"Well, okay, but I think you should just let me say this one thing."

I shrugged. She was probably going to pester me

until I gave in. I figured I might as well get it over with.

"I know this must be rough for you," she began.

"It's not rough," I said. "It's ridiculous."

"So, why don't you find out for yourself, just to be sure."

"I'm already sure."

"Then what would be the harm in … contacting your father?"

"That should be easy," I said with a sneer, "considering that I haven't seen or heard from him since I was four years old, and I have no idea where he lives. He could be in jail, or dead for all I know."

"Have you ever *tried* to find him?"

"No."

"Well, what could it hurt? To try, I mean."

"There's no point," I said.

"There *is*! He's your *father*."

I was going to argue, but the way her voice sounded when she said *father* got to me. It was like she'd hauled off and sucker-punched me in the gut. I had a hard time getting a breath.

"You can use my computer if you want," she said. "Check out Canada 411 and some other sites."

"What's the worst thing that could happen, just looking?" she asked when we'd walked another half block without me answering.

"Okay, okay!" I said. "But, if we find him, I'm not calling him then and there. I'll think about it *if* we get anything."

"Sure. No pressure," she said quickly. "You can decide all that later on. When you're ready."

When I was ready.

I wondered if I would ever be ready.

chapter twenty-four

Sounds of aircraft gunfire met us when Lavender opened the door to her place. Her dad was in a big easy chair with a bowl of popcorn on his lap and a bottle of pop on the end table beside him. There were also wrappers from a Snickers bar and a couple of ice cream sandwiches.

"Dad likes to snack when he watches movies," Lavender said.

"Hey kids," he said, pressing pause on the DVD player. "You come to see the show?"

"No, Dad, we're just going to do some research in my room," she told him.

"Okey-dokey," he said. "Don't forget to leave the door open."

"I *know*," she said, reddening. "You don't have to say that every time."

"Sorry about that," she said when we were out of her father's earshot. "My parents are *so* weird!"

"It's okay," I said. "He's just looking out for you."

"I suppose. But they don't make sense, you know? I mean, you were here this afternoon and no one else was home — at least for part of the time. And that was okay. But I can't shut the door if we're in my room — even when my dad is right here. It's just stupid."

She was right, the rule didn't seem logical, but I had other things on my mind right then. As if she knew what I was thinking, Lavender turned to her desk and clicked on the mouse to wake up the screen.

"C'mon, c'mon," she said, sliding into the chair. Then she flashed me a quick smile. "Don't mind me. I am *so* impatient about waiting."

"Should I make a mental note of that?" I asked, noticing how small and delicate the back of her head looked.

"Wouldn't hurt." She laughed. "I'm not really that bad, though."

While she talked, she moved the mouse to bring up her favourites and I saw that she had a folder of sites for locating people and places. She clicked on one and then turned to me questioningly.

"What's your dad's first name?"

"Steve. Or Steven, I guess. With a *v*."

She typed that in, asked if his last name was Delancy, too, and added that. She searched all across Canada.

In novels, it's always the very last place that gets results. Just when hope is almost gone, there it is. It didn't work that way for me. On the first search she did, Lavender turned up not one but two Steve Delancys. One of them was in British Columbia, the other was in Brampton.

"Think one of these guys is him?"

"I dunno. Probably."

"Think it's the guy in Brampton?"

"Could be either one." But the thought had hit me hard. Was it possible that my father was that nearby — maybe had been all those years — and hadn't once bothered to get in touch?

"That would be fantastic!" Lavender said. She jumped up and hugged me, kissed me kind of half on the mouth half on the cheek, and started dancing around holding my hands and trying to drag me along with her.

"Right. Fantastic," I said. I extracted myself from her grip and stepped back a few feet. She stopped twirling and looked at me. I saw confusion on her face, then hurt. She pulled her gaze away, let it wander past me without focusing on anything in particular.

"Could be that *neither* of these guys is my father," I

said. I didn't know why, but I felt angry, and it was taking her in.

"I, well, you ..." Her voice trailed away helplessly. She plunked down on her bed.

"I'll just write the information down for now," I said. I was being a jerk and I knew it. At the same time, part of me wanted to smooth things over with her before I messed up totally.

"Paper's in the top drawer on the side," she said. She waved a hand indifferently toward the desk.

I opened the drawer and pulled out a sheet of paper, reached for a big old coffee mug full of pens, pencils, and markers, snagged a pen and copied out the details of the two Steve Delancys. As I did, I was acutely aware that I might be writing down my father's address and phone number.

"Are you going to tell your sister about this?" Lavender asked.

"I dunno. Maybe," I said.

The truth was: I hadn't even thought about it. It seemed wrong to keep it from her, but at the same time I knew if I gave this to Lynn she might tell Mom about it right away. I didn't think that would help matters and I sure didn't want to be forced into anything before I was ready.

I had the strange feeling that if I made a mistake

now, it might close the door for good. When the time came that I got in touch with my father, it had to be on my terms. No one else's.

If, that was, he even wanted to be contacted.

That thought hit me like a sidewinder and I wondered why it hadn't occurred to me before.

Maybe my father would hang up without talking at all. Actually, when I ran it through my head, that was the most likely case scenario! A man who'd first abused and then abandoned his kids twelve years earlier was liable to dismiss a phone call as easily as he would shoo away a fly.

"He might not want anything to do with me — or Lynn," I said out loud.

Lavender looked a bit startled. Of course she hadn't been privy to the thoughts racing around in my head, so the comment had come out of the blue for her.

"He *probably* won't want anything to do with us," I revised.

"What makes you say that?"

I filled her in on what I'd been thinking and I could see that the idea alarmed her. Scared her even.

"You're not going to know until you call," she finally said. Her voice was really soft and I knew she was still confused from the way I'd acted a few moments ago.

I didn't answer right away because scenes were

running around in my head. I could picture him telling me to get lost, maybe denying that he was the right guy, or rudely asking me what I wanted.

The more I envisioned that kind of thing happening, the more likely it seemed to me that it would work out that way. And the thought of it made me madder than I'd been in a long, long time.

I looked down at the paper in my hand, noticed that it was shaking, and forced myself to take a couple of deep breaths to steady myself.

"You know what," I said, "I think I *will* call him. I think I'll call him right *now*."

Lavender's eyes got wide and scared. I'd put money down that she wanted to suggest this might not be the best time — after all her nagging earlier! But she said nothing. She simply grabbed her bag off the floor, reached inside, and passed me her phone.

I didn't hesitate, didn't pause to think of what I was going to say or how I was going to say it. I punched in the numbers for the Brampton guy and lifted the phone to my ear.

It rang three times before anyone picked it up.

"Hello?" It was a kid's voice — I couldn't tell if it was a girl or boy.

"Uh, yeah," I said, wondering if I'd dialled wrong. "Is Steve Delancy there?"

"Uh-huh. Just a minute." The phone clattered on a hard surface and I heard the kid calling in the background.

"Dad! Pho-one!"

Dad?

I would have hung up right then, if my whole body hadn't frozen with shock.

"Hello?"

"Is this Steve Delancy?" I asked when I could get my voice to co-operate again.

"Yes."

Then I didn't know what to say. This might not even be the right guy. But how could I eliminate him without asking questions? And what could I ask that wouldn't sound bizarre if he was a total stranger?

"I, uh," I faltered. "Did you ever have, uh, I mean, me and my sister ..."

"Who's calling?" he asked. His voice had taken on an edge that I couldn't quite identify.

"I think I have the wrong person," I said.

I heard him take a deep breath.

"Is this ..." his voice trailed off to a whisper but I was almost positive I heard my name at the end, though it was barely audible.

I said nothing, which is what I owed him.

"Porter?" he repeated. It was stronger this time. Hopeful.

"Yeah." It came out harsh and angry. He started to speak again, and I heard the word *son* as I pulled the phone away from my ear and snapped it shut.

chapter twenty-five

I had never thought I wanted things to be different than they were, but stuff was churning around in me and suddenly nothing seemed clear anymore. It was all there, pushing up to the surface — things that weren't even supposed to exist — disappointment and buried wishes and hope I hadn't known I felt.

Okay, I might have had a slight idea, now and then, that there was something missing, but I hadn't *cared* about it. I think I'd have noticed if I'd been walking around with this big empty space in me, just longing for a father to fill it.

"I couldn't care less," I said.

"What?"

I hadn't realized I'd spoken out loud until Lavender's startled question brought me back into focus. It wasn't fair, but it irritated me that she was there, watching and listening.

"Nothing."

"That was him, wasn't it? That guy was your father!"

"If you can call him that."

"So, what happened?"

"Nothing happened. I just realized I had nothing to say to him."

She spent a good fifteen minutes trying to persuade me to call back. All it did was make me want to leave. I came up with a lame excuse and almost felt guilty when her face told me she knew it was a lie. Still, that was the end of her attempt to talk me into something I had no interest in doing.

To be honest, I wasn't sure why I'd called in the first place. I thought this over as I walked aimlessly, not ready to go home and too restless to be around anyone else.

It took four more days of thinking, avoiding everyone, and letting my thoughts burn and churn before I was both curious and angry enough to call him again.

There were things I wanted to tell him, things that had circled in my head over the past few days — hard, cutting words. I knew I had to say them, even though it wasn't likely he'd even care. He'd proven that long ago.

At the very least, I was going to demand some answers. Whether I'd get the truth was another thing, but I figured I'd be able to tell.

I started to dial the number from my place a few times but it was too risky. That would give him my number — assuming he didn't already have it. There would be big problems if he called there sometime and Mom answered. Seemed foolish to take that chance, so I presented myself at Lavender's door like I hadn't ignored her calls for the last few days, and told her I'd needed thinking time, which was true.

She wasn't happy. I hadn't expected her to be. But I knew I had a sure "in" and I used it.

"I've decided you were right. And I'm going to call him back."

"Really?" Just like that her face was lit up and smiling.

"Yeah."

"When?" Her hand fluttered up to her throat. "Now? Did you come here to share it with me?"

"Yeah, sort of." I couldn't quite look at her. "Is it all right if I call from your room? For privacy?"

Of course it was. She went with me to (as she put it) get things ready. That apparently meant clearing the desk and putting a pen and paper out.

"Just in case," she said. I had no idea what the 'in case' might be, and I didn't ask.

Lavender insisted on bringing me a glass of water, too, and just before she left she sat a box of Kleenex on the desk. As soon as the door closed behind her I threw them over my shoulder and heard the box slap the wall before it went down.

I had the number with me but I'd looked at it enough times that I remembered it. I grabbed the phone and pressed the number keys.

I hoped that kid didn't answer this time.

Two rings. Three. I decided to hang up after four.

"Hello?"

It was him. Steve Delancy.

"It's Porter," I said curtly, pleased with the hard, blunt sound of my voice.

"I'm glad you called, Porter."

It threw me just a little, how calm and quiet his voice was.

"I was thinking about, uh, getting together."

"Anytime," he said, without skipping a beat. "I can come whenever you want."

"Now?" I said.

"Absolutely," he said. "I've been waiting for this call for twelve years."

You haven't been waiting for *this* call, I thought. I didn't say that — he'd know soon enough that this wasn't going to be some kind of happy reunion.

"Okay," I said. I told him I'd meet him at Suleiman's restaurant and gave him the address for his GPS. He said he'd be there in less than an hour.

We said goodbye and I closed the phone. I stared at it for a few minutes like it had done this thing all on its own. I almost called back and told him I'd changed my mind but I knew I needed to get this over with. Things weren't going to be normal again until I put it behind me.

I picked up the box of Kleenex I'd thrown and put it on the desk before going to look for Lavender. I found her curled up on the couch, facing the television. She turned when I came in, jumped up and hurried over, her face questioning.

"I have to go," I said, even though I had lots of time. I nodded slightly toward the kitchen, where her dad was making something to eat.

Lavender grabbed my arm and pulled me out the door, stopping in the hallway just outside.

"What happened?" she demanded.

"I'm meeting up with him."

"*No way*! That is *awesome*!" She threw her arms around me and gave me a quick, hard hug, then stepped back and looked at my face. "Are you excited?"

"I really don't feel anything right now," I said, surprised that it was true.

"I bet you're kind of in shock," she said. "Just look at everything that's happened in a few days. You saw your dad's pictures, then we followed that guy to his place, and now you've talked to your father and you're going to see him."

I tried to smile but my jaw felt too tight. I told her again that I had to go.

Lavender offered to walk with me to Suleiman's. I said thanks but I really wanted to be by myself for a while. I had to get my head together.

She understood, or said she did. I've noticed it's not always the same thing with girls, but I kissed her and she kissed back normal, which seemed like a good sign. It wouldn't have mattered anyway — I really couldn't be around anyone right then.

I wondered again why I didn't feel more anger. I decided Lavender was right — I was a bit in shock.

When I got to Suleiman's, I didn't go in. There was no way I could make myself sit there until he showed up. Instead, I paced a bit up and down the street and wondered if I'd recognize him after seeing the pictures the other day. He must have changed a certain amount in the years that had passed since then.

I should have asked him what kind of car he'd be driving. That would have been a help. After all, he didn't know what I looked like, either.

That realization made me mad. And it was right then that I felt a hand on my shoulder. I shrugged it off automatically and turned to see him standing there smiling.

"Porter," he said.

Dad.

"Yeah," I said. I wondered how he'd known who I was, but then I could see I looked a lot like him.

"I've waited a long time for this day," he said. His eyes were starting to fill up. I barely managed to keep from asking him right then and there where all this fatherly emotion had been all the years he never bothered with me.

"Did you want to go inside," he asked, nodding toward Suleiman's, "or maybe take a drive, find somewhere a bit more private to talk?"

I said that was a good idea. The chance of getting some straight answers out of him would be better somewhere that other people couldn't overhear.

chapter twenty-six

It was so strange, being in the car next to him, driving along. I bet a million other sons were sitting next to their fathers while they drove somewhere right at that moment. And for them it was just a normal thing to do. For me, it was totally surreal, like something happening to someone else.

I've never been hypnotized but I bet it feels pretty close to the trance-like state I found myself in. All of the questions and anger I'd been trying to sort out quieted, like they were resting, as we drove. A totally peaceful, relaxed feeling flowed through me, and I found myself sinking back against the upholstery and watching my father's every movement as he drove. For some reason I got so drowsy that a couple of times I almost fell asleep.

I think he must have been aware that I was staring at him non-stop. For sure he saw that every time he glanced over at me (which was often) I was looking right at him. I didn't care if it looked rude or stupid, I just let myself gawk, unembarrassed. He'd disappeared out of my life for twelve years — I figured I had the right to take a good look.

He didn't say anything just then, except to ask if I was hungry or thirsty. I said I could use some water and he stopped at a gas station and got us each a couple of bottles.

He pulled back out onto the street and headed south, then took an exit onto the Gardiner. Before long we'd stopped at a place along the water — a little park-type spot with benches and trees.

We got out of the car like that was something we'd decided in advance, and walked along the path to a fairly secluded bench. There was no one else around, which was good, and even if someone came by we still had some degree of privacy.

I turned to face him, took a gulp of water, and waited. I'd decided that I'd let him go ahead and talk first, see what he had to say for himself, and then hit him with the questions.

"I can't tell you how happy I am that you called," he said when he finally spoke. "I've waited and prayed for this day ever since your mother and I separated."

He stopped to clear his throat. "Lynn ... how is she? Does she know about this?"

"Lynn's fine," I said. "And no, she doesn't know I called you."

"Are you two still close?"

"We're okay," I said. "What do you mean, *still*?"

"You were always playing together when you were little," he answered. "You used to pester her until she'd get down on all fours and let you ride around on her back. Then, you'd holler "Giddy-Up" and kind of bounce up and down because she wasn't wild enough for you. You liked to ride on my back because I'd do the bucking bronco thing."

He smiled sadly and his eyes drifted back in time. "You were a little wild man when you were small. Used to practically give your mother a heart attack by launching yourself off the furniture — the couch, coffee table, bed. You crashed into the wall once and never made so much as a peep about it — just jumped to your feet and headed for the chair to get up and go again."

"How old was I?"

"I'd say you started with the wild-man stunts around eighteen months, and kept them up ... well, for as long as I was around. I didn't get much in terms of information about what you were doing after that. I guess you know things didn't go smoothly between your mother and me after I moved out."

"I know she hates you for what you *did* to us," I said. I looked at him hard and waited to see how he'd react.

He hesitated before he spoke again. "I was hoping you'd still have some good memories."

"Of you? How could I after what you did to us?" My voice was flat but I could feel the anger surging back.

"Porter, I don't know what you think you remember, but I promise you that I never did anything to hurt you or Lynn."

"Don't you dare call my mother a liar," I said through clenched teeth. It was all I could do not to get up and walk away, but I reminded myself I wasn't through with him — yet.

"I don't know what to say, Porter," he told me. "All I can tell you is that your mom was hurt and angry when we broke up. I expected everything to be worked out like it would be in most cases where a marriage has ended, but it didn't happen that way. I was awarded visitation — and I've lost track of the times I went back to court trying to enforce it — but I never got so much as one weekend with you and Lynn. And the worst thing was that you and your sister were put under tremendous pressure by the whole situation.

"Nothing that was ordered in court helped — everything spun more and more out-of-control until I felt I had no choice but to step away. Nothing I did worked, and eventually I ran out of things to try. The day finally came that I gave up — not on you and Lynn, but on expecting anything to change through normal channels. From then on, I just prayed about it and trusted that it would all work out somehow, someday."

His tone and everything seemed so sincere that I almost bought it, so it was a good thing I'd gone over the things I wanted to say earlier. I wasn't going to be taken in and fooled, like some little kid. I had questions to ask, and he was going to hear them.

"Yeah? So then why didn't you ever send us anything, or pay support?" I asked.

"I sent gifts and letters to both of you, in care of your Aunt Jean, until about three years ago, when they started coming back. I guess Jean had moved then and when she did I lost the one place I could still send things for you. Your mother had a court order blocking me from having your address.

"As for support — I've never missed a payment. I assume you've been told otherwise."

"I never got any presents or letters from you," I said.

He paused. "The last thing I sent you was a Play-station. That was for Christmas about three years back. Some of the other things I can remember are a Blue Jays baseball jersey, roller blades, a compass and binoculars —"

"I don't know about any of that," I interrupted, but my stomach was churning. Everything he'd listed I'd gotten but … those gifts had been from Mom. I pushed away my confusion by saying, "And what about child support? Mom told us you *never* paid a cent to support us."

"I never *missed* a support payment," he said. "Not once. And I was only too happy to be able to pay it — to contribute *something* to you and Lynn — since I wasn't able to be with you."

"Then I guess you'd have some kind of proof of that," I said, unable to hide my disgust. I knew he was lying, and I didn't care that my voice made that clear to him.

"Sure I do," he said. "They give me receipts every month. In fact, I think I have one in my wallet."

We looked at each other and I could see he was holding his ground, wanting me to believe him without seeing the receipt. He was going to force me to demand it.

"So, show me," I said, but it made me feel as though I'd lost something by saying it.

He reached into his pocket without ever taking his eyes off me, pulled out his wallet, and flipped it open. He glanced down, found a white stub of paper sticking out of one of many slits, slid it out, and passed it to me without opening it.

I took it and unfolded it because for some reason I had to play this thing out right to the end. It was a receipt from the courthouse for child support, dated that month. I realized at that moment that he was telling the truth, and that he'd paid every month all along.

My mother had lied. She'd lied about support payments and she'd lied and pretended the gifts he'd sent were from her.

My mouth was dry and I tilted up my water bottle and drained it before passing the receipt back.

"You never even tried to see me … us," I said. The anger was forced now, though, and sliding off fast. Or, rather, it was turning around and heading somewhere else.

"Porter, I'm sorry you think that, and I can't change the way things were, but I swear I did the best I could. Maybe there was something more, something I didn't try, but short of kidnapping you, there was no way I could think of that would have let me see you when you were small. The two of you were trained to say things. You told social workers and psychologists I'd abused you. You told me you hated me and never wanted to see me again. Once, your sister even made a terrible claim that I'd touched her inappropriately, of all the sick things! Thankfully that was proven false during the investigation, or I might have been charged and jailed."

His voice rose just a little in anger and anguish as he recited the events from the past. "There was only so much I was willing to put the two of you through

— only so many lies I'd see you coached to tell, only so much pressure I could stand to see you under. It was clear the courts were blind and the social workers untrained in that particular area. Two of the psychologists saw that you were being poisoned against me, and they made some recommendations to the court, but the court orders that resulted weren't worth the paper they were written on. Your mother kept sidestepping, making up new stories about what a monster I was ... and dragging you two along through it all. It was so unfair to you and Lynn ... so hard on you. In the end, I had to stop trying and just have faith that it would all right itself some day."

He talked for a while longer, until I realized I didn't need to hear anymore. Sanning had been right. I *had* wanted to see my father. There had been questions and doubts in me that I hadn't even known were there, memories of the truth that were pushing their way to the surface.

I stopped him, holding my hand up and saying, "I guess I always knew the truth on some level. I don't know why it wasn't clear all along."

It took him a few minutes to be able to speak again.

"How could it be clear? Two beautiful children were taken from someone who loved them more than life itself, and programmed to think he had hurt them and that they couldn't trust him. That's pretty heavy stuff for a child to sort through."

The word *child* triggered one of the questions I'd made a mental note to ask him.

"You have another kid?" I asked.

"Oh ... yes. You and Lynn have another sister you've never met. I remarried seven years ago and my wife and I had Nicole the following year."

I let that sink in. A six-year-old sister. Nicole.

"Does she know about me and Lynn?"

"Of course. She's always asking me *when* she'll *finally* get to meet you." He said it with an emphasis that I knew was hers. Nicole's. My little sister.

"What's your wife's name?"

"Amelia. She's a good person. You'll like her."

It was after that that we *really* started to talk. Dad told me a lot about himself and his new family, and I told him about me and Lynn. I couldn't believe it when he glanced at his watch and said it was almost four in the morning.

"Will your mother be waiting up for you?"

"Naw, she'll be sleeping." I wasn't worried about Mom, anyway. There were things to straighten out, but I didn't even want to think about all that tonight.

Knowing what time it was seemed to have an effect on both of us, though, and we were soon yawning. Dad put his arm around my shoulder and said maybe we'd better head back. I was okay with that because this was just the beginning.

On the way home I recalled something. I asked him if he remembered the day outside the daycare, when I'd been coached to say I hated him.

He did.

"It wasn't true, Dad," I said. "It was *never* true."

"I know that, Son," he said. "I always knew it."

chapter twenty-seven

It was Lynn who found the letters.

Mom had been hanging around the apartment and I knew she'd sniffed something out — probably because of us going through all her stuff the day we were looking for the key to her cabinet. She didn't ask about it, but it was easy to see she was watching us, waiting to see if we might give anything away.

Even though I'd been out late the night before, I was up early that morning, my head too full of everything to let me sleep in. Lynn got up not long afterward, and once she'd had her breakfast I gave her a signal that I needed to talk to her.

"I think I'll head over to Tack's place, see what's up," I said, lying for Mom's benefit. I caught Lynn's eye and pointed down, hoping she'd know to meet me in the lobby.

It was about twenty minutes before she joined me, bursting out of the elevator with a panicked look on her face.

"I thought for sure you'd be gone," she said breathlessly. "What's going on?"

"Come on," I said. "We can't talk here."

We slipped out the back entrance, just in case Mom was watching out the window, and went through to the street behind our building. From there we made our way to the park and, finding the few benches there occupied, sat on the grass under a maple tree.

I started slowly, giving her time to take it all in. She kept interrupting, asking me questions that made me repeat what I'd just said. It was almost comical.

"You called our father?" she said, right after I'd told her that exact thing.

"Yeah, I called him."

"You called *our father*?" Then, like that needed clarifying: "Our *real* dad?"

Eventually I got through the whole story with her. She sat very still, looking at the ground, her head suspended forward over her knees. She tugged at a few blades of grass, then she cried silently for a bit.

"He drew funny faces on balloons," she said, without looking at me. "Do you remember?"

Something flashed forward from the memories I'd

had to freeze out, but it was gone before I could get a solid image.

"Maybe a little bit," I said.

"How could she?" Lynn said then. "How could she do this to us?"

"I've been wondering that, too. And why."

"I mean it, Porter. *How could she?*" Her voice rose, caught in her throat, then turned into a moan, and more tears.

"Take it easy, Lynn." I said a few other things to try to calm her and even went so far as attempting to put an arm around her shoulders, but she shrugged it off and rose to her feet. In an instant transformation, she became red-faced and ugly with anger.

"She's going to tell me *right now* why she did this to us!" she said through clenched teeth.

I went along with her, making half-hearted (and futile) attempts to talk to her while she stomped toward home. I'd never seen Lynn this mad before and as small as she was, there was something terrible and frightening in the way she looked — and even in the way she moved.

It wasn't until we were in the elevator on the way up to our apartment that I was able to make her hear me.

"Just don't do anything she can get you for," I begged. Mom had called the police on Lynn once when there'd been a bit of shoving back and forth. Nothing had come of that, but I knew there could be big trouble if Lynn so much as touched her.

"Don't worry," she said, breathing a bit more normally.

It was hard not to worry, especially when we got inside and Lynn exploded with a stream of name-calling and accusations. It took Mom a good three or four minutes to even *start* reacting.

"I knew this would happen someday," she said, trying to yell over Lynn. "He got to you, didn't he? Got to you and filled your head with lies. Well, I—"

"*SHUT UP*," Lynn screamed. "*YOU SHUT YOUR LYING MOUTH.*"

Mom ventured a glance at me to see if she might find someone on her side. I guess she didn't see any sympathy in my eyes because she backed down and stayed silent while Lynn went on for the next few minutes.

It might have lasted longer but she stopped raving in mid-sentence and turned to me, her face wild with fury.

"Where's that key? I bet there's other stuff in her cabinet that she doesn't want us to see."

Mom looked *really* scared when she heard that. She stood up and took a few faltering steps toward the hallway but stopped when Lynn spun around and faced her.

"You just try and stop me," she said. "Go ahead and try."

Lynn's voice had gone totally calm and quiet, which, in a way, was scarier than the screaming. Mom's mouth moved, fishlike, but nothing came out. Panic was written all over her face but even then I could see her searching for something to say.

I turned away, unable to find so much as a hint of pity for her, and followed my sister down the hall, stopping in my room to get the key.

I handed it to Lynn and stood at her side as she slid it into the keyhole and turned, pulled the drawers open, and started pulling things out and throwing them on the bed behind us.

It was surprising how much those two drawers held. There were all kinds of documents and court papers, Mom's income tax returns, cards, pictures and, nestled underneath everything else in the top drawer, neat stacks of letters tied in bundles.

Lynn snatched out the top bundle with a little cry and clutched it to her. I saw there were several other stacks addressed to her underneath and to the right of those, twin bundles with my name on them.

Letters. Dozens and dozens of letters. And every one of them had been opened.

"This is *my* room!" Mom, now in the doorway, did her best to put authority and indignation into her voice, but all she sounded was scared.

"And these are *our* letters," I snapped. Then, curious, "Why didn't you just throw them out?"

"I was *protecting* you," she said. Her eyes begged me to believe her. "I didn't want you getting confused or upset."

"So, why keep them?" I repeated.

"In case ..." She hesitated. "In case anything ever happened to me. I couldn't stand the idea of you in foster homes. I thought that *anything* would be better than that."

There were things I would have liked to say to that, but I somehow managed to hold them in. Mom misunderstood my silence.

"You know, Porter," she said, her face pathetic with hope, "you can't believe anything that monster says to you."

I turned away from her and saw that Lynn had sunk onto the edge of the bed and was reading one of her letters. Tears streamed down her face and her shoulders shook. She looked so small.

"Lynn," I said. "Come on, let's get out of here."

She looked up, her eyes confused, like she was trying to focus on something after coming in from bright sunshine.

"I'm going to call Dad to come and get us," I said.
Dad.

"Won't he be working right now?"

"Yeah, but he'll come. He gave me his card with his work and cell phone numbers."

"You're not calling *him* from my phone," Mom said. Her last pitiful attempt at control.

I shrugged, grabbed the rest of my letters, and walked, with my sister, down the hall and out the door.

Behind us, we could hear Mom yelling that we were fools if we thought we could trust our father, and that we'd be sorry if we didn't turn around right that moment.

We kept walking.

epilogue

If you ever want to plan a surprise party for someone, don't let my little sister, Nicole, in on it. Believe me, you'd have a better chance of keeping it under wraps if you put it in the paper.

I knew they would do something for my graduation, but I'd thought it would be along the lines of a family dinner out. We almost always go out for birthdays and other special occasions.

The first hint that it was going to be a party instead came when Nicole started guarding the deep freeze.

"Don't look in here!" she'd yell, throwing herself across the front of it.

"Yeah, okay," I told her. I didn't give it much thought, since doing weird things isn't exactly unusual for her.

But other things started adding up — like the way she'd yell, "Oh, hi, *Porter*!" when I'd start to walk into a room. It wouldn't have taken a towering genius to know something was up.

Still, I played ignorant and didn't even crack a smile when Dad asked me to drive out to a place in Caledon to pick up some garden plants for Amelia.

Of course, when I got back the house was very quiet — that is, until I walked into the living room. I did my best to look shocked when everyone yelled "Surprise!" and I think they bought it.

"We *surprised* you!" Nicole giggled, dancing around in circles beside me.

In spite of her numerous giveaways, it was true. I *was* surprised — not that there was a party, but at some of the people who were there.

Like Andrew Daniels, my old probation officer. Dad had been in touch with him, and we had all gone for lunch downtown at The Pickle Barrel not too long after I'd moved to my father's house. (Dad wanted — or maybe needed — to thank as many people as he could who had been there for me or helped me out during the years he'd kept away.) Still, I hadn't expected Daniels to come to a graduation party for me.

He shook my hand and said he was proud of me.

"Yeah. Thanks, man. *Really*," I said. I could tell, the way he nodded that he knew exactly what I meant.

Lester and Addie Phelps were there, both of them

beaming from ear to ear. I'd never made it to another one of their "hot dog and Freshie" parties, but they'd been right at the top of the list of people Dad and I had taken out for dinner.

I talked to them for a while and was proud to introduce them to my grandparents. (It seemed strange that I'd known the Phelpses for so much longer than my dad's parents.) The four of them got talking about the way things were years ago, the way old people do, and I moved on to other guests. There were more relatives I'd met since moving there, and some neighbours, and a few people from church. We go every Sunday and it still seems a bit strange, but there's a nice feeling there, a kind of warm, family feeling, and I like that part.

When I was getting something to eat a bit later I saw that Addie had brought some of her famous oatmeal cookies. Amelia had made a lot of fancy things to eat (finger foods, I guess she calls them) but she'd cleared room on one of the platters for the cookies. I snagged a couple and saw Addie's eyes crinkle with a smile.

Lynn and her new boyfriend, Barry, were there, with Nicole pretty much tagging along behind them. (Nicole is like a one-person entourage to Lynn, who she thinks is glamorous and cool. She also says Barry is cute, but I can't quite get my brain to let that kind of talk in when it's coming from my eight-year-old sister.)

Amelia darted around everywhere, snapping pictures, telling us to never mind her, she wanted all natural shots and we should just act like she was invisible.

"That's a bit difficult when someone is half blinding you with a flash," Dad pointed out.

"Don't be such a *boy*," she told him.

You might have noticed that I didn't mention Tack being at the party. That's because he was having his own graduation thing the same night. He came over that weekend, though, and we went canoeing and stayed at my grandparent's cabin on the Kawartha Lakes.

Lavender wasn't there, either. We're still friends, but we didn't keep going out. I talk to her once in a while and part of me hopes we'll eventually get back together, but I'm not counting on it. There was a lot I really liked about her but it turned out her drug use wasn't as harmless as she'd believed. It got between us fast, and when we realized that, she decided to quit.

I don't think Lavender ever saw getting high as a problem until she tried to give it up — for us — and found out it was a lot harder than she'd expected it to be. I could have handled that okay, but she started trying to hide it from me.

After living with lies my whole life, that was more than I could deal with. We agreed to stay friends, and like I said, we talk now and then, but that's it for now.

And, of course, my mother didn't come, though Amelia invited her. To tell the truth, that was fine with me.

Dad keeps telling me that it's important for me to forgive Mom. He says we should pity her more than anything because she had to be really sick to do what she did to us. Maybe he's right and the day might come that I will, but right now I can't find it in me.

I *have* tried to talk to her on the phone a few times but it's just pointless. She still denies what she did and I don't think that will ever change. I get the same spew of lies and persuasions, like it's not too late to convince me of stuff she could never *entirely* make me believe over twelve years.

Dad says maybe she can't face what she took from me and Lynn, but I know it's not that. She still thinks she has a chance to "win" and she doesn't care how much anyone else loses in the process.

Lynn went back to live with Mom after she and Conor broke up for good. I could hardly believe it, after she'd been so furious, but she said she couldn't stand seeing Mom so broken up and alone.

That lasted a week and a half, and they haven't talked since. Lynn lived here for a while, too, but said she just couldn't live with Amelia. It wasn't that they actually fought or anything, but Lynn said she felt like she was being judged. I have no idea what she meant by that, and with Lynn I may never know.

Anyway, she got a job and moved into an apartment in Scarborough with a couple of other girls. She's doing okay, in general, and even talks about going back to school sometime. I hope she does. I think that, being older, she got a lot more dumped on her than I did, and that's probably made it harder for her to adjust.

In a way, Lynn is a sort of restless type. Still, she shows up here whenever there's any kind of family thing going on and I think she's starting to feel like she belongs.

I am, too, but it's not as easy as I thought it would be. Things got on track fairly fast with Dad — that part was okay. Amelia and Nicole and the house and all the changes, that doesn't seem one hundred percent part of my life. Not yet.

We went to the zoo last summer — Dad, Amelia, Lynn, Nicole, and I. I thought I might catch more buried memories there — like being on my father's shoulders while we raced giraffes.

That happens sometimes, bits and pieces of the past still sneak through and they're like old photos, a bit hazy but with faces and places you can still recognize. I look at them until they start to blur, trying to grab every possible detail.

But at the zoo that day, even though I tried to open myself up to let in any memories that might be lurking, there was nothing.

We talked later on, Dad and I, and I told him I was a bit disappointed that I didn't recover any more memories that day.

And he said, "Maybe not, Son. But on the other hand, you *made* some."

acknowledgements

Special thanks to Amber Murray, the real inventor of "Roastin' the Ghetto Bootie," the dance performed by Lavender Dean in this story.

And, as always, I am grateful for so many wonderful individuals in my life and world:

My husband, partner and best friend, Brent.

My parents, Bob and Pauline Russell. My son Anthony, his wife Maria, and daughters Emilee, Ericka, and Veronicka. My daughter Pamela and her husband David Jardine. My brothers and their families: Danny and Gail; Andrew, Shelley, Bryce, and Drew. My "other" family: Ron and Phoebe Sherrard, Ron Sherrard and Dr. Kiran Pure, Bruce and Roxanne Mullin, and Karen Sherrard.

My sixth grade teacher, the late Alf Lower, whose influence lives on.

Friends: Janet Aube, Jimmy Allain, Karen Arseneault, Darlene Cowton, Angi Garofolo, Karen Gauvin, Eric Fallon, Rosemary Fowlie, Gail and Paul Jardine, John Hambrook, Sandra Henderson, Thelma and Lorne Livingston, Mary Matchett, Johnnye Montgomery, Colleen Power, Marsha Skrypuch, Linda Stevens, Pam Sturgeon, Bonnie Thompson, and Beatrice Tucker.

The terrific team at the Dundurn Group.

Readers! Hearing from you is the best part of writing, and I love getting your letters and emails. In recent months, the following young people have taken the time to get in touch: Miranda Augustine, Michael Bain, Troy Bartja, Travis Bender, Brianne Bentley, Cam Bierling, Jared Braun, Sarah Crummey, Adrienne Rose Deeley, Hayden Desjardins, Rebekah Doiron, Keily Forster, Robbie Hamilton, Katie Howarth, Olivia Jones, Derica Lafrance, Julia Latuskie, Sisi Liu, Katherine Luymes, Desiree Marleau, Justin Mattinson, Stephanie Middleton, Alisa Murray, Keirstin Anne Murray, Shahama Najeeb, Michelle Nuttley, Alexandria Osolky, Jacqulyn Osolky, Archana Premkumar, Alexis Piercey, Courtney Pitre, Taylor Pringle, Alexandria Reid, Amanda Smith, Kolby Smith, Elise Steveson,

watcher

Olivia Thompson, Lucy Wang, David Wiercigroch,
Teresa Yin, Lisa Yoon, and Molly Meiling Zhai.
You are the voice of tomorrow. Speak wisely and well.
Speak truth.

ALSO BY VALERIE SHERRARD

Three Million Acres of Flame
978-1-55002-727-3
$12.99

For Skye Haverill and her family, it begins as an ordinary day. But in the annals of Canadian history, October 7, 1825, is the date of one of our greatest national disasters. Family strife quickly becomes irrelevant when the Haverills and their community are caught up in the Miramichi Fire, the largest blaze in North American history. As the family and the town struggle through the disaster and the devastating aftermath, all must find a way to rebuild homes and relationships.

Speechless
978-1-55002-701-3
$12.99

When his teacher announces that it's time for the yearly class speeches, Griffin Maxwell starts to sweat. Until his best friend comes up with a solution — one so simple it just has to work! But neither boy can begin to predict the bizarre chain of events that will be set in motion when Griffin goes along with the idea. From squaring off with the school bully to reading a teacher's private letters, Griffin will have to face things he never imagined, and all without saying a word!

RECENT NOVELS FOR YOUNG PEOPLE

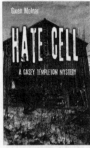